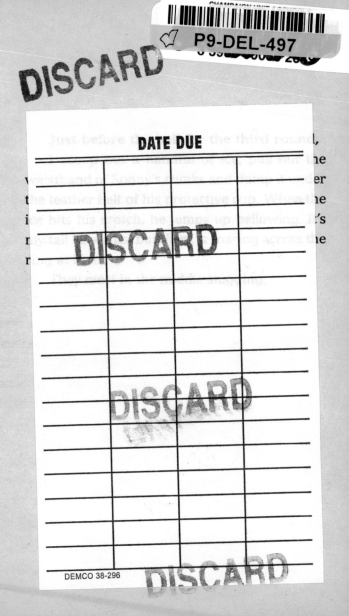

DATE DUE

Just before the bell for the third round,
someone slips a handful of ice chill into the
waistband of Sonny's trunks, way deep, up under
the leather belt of his protective cup. When the
ice hits his crotch, he jumps up bellowing. It's
my turn to laugh now, me, barreling across the
ring at him . . .

They meet in the middle, snapping.

DEMCO 38-296

THE CHIEF

Robert Lipsyte

▩ HarperTrophy®
An Imprint of HarperCollins*Publishers*

The Chief
Copyright © 1993 by Robert M. Lipsyte

Library of Congress Cataloging-in-Publication Data
Lipsyte, Robert.
The chief / by Robert Lipsyte.
p.   cm.
Summary: On the verge of having a shot at the heavyweight
boxing championship, nineteen-year-old Sonny Bear finds him-
self with conflicting loyalties when trouble erupts on his reser-
vation over the construction of a new gambling casino.
Sequel to: The brave.
ISBN 0-06-447097-0 (pbk.)
1. Indians of North America—Juvenile fiction. [1.Indians of
North America—Fiction. 2. Boxing—Fiction.] I. Title.
PZ7.L67Ci 1993   92-54502
[Fic]—dc20   CIP
                                                             AC

Typography by Henrietta Stern
✦
First Harper Trophy edition, 1995
Visit us on the World Wide Web!
www.harperteen.com

I don't mind being the butt, if it gets us over. "Words are like punches, a new—"

"Shut up," says Alfred. "Scared, Sonny?"

"That don't work no more," says Sonny. "Wake up. Elston Hubbard's fighting in Vegas for a title shot and I'm here in Woptown . . ."

"Portuguese Americans," says Jake, "and that kind of talk . . ."

". . . going nowhere."

". . . don't get us anywhere," says Jake.

"Got to keep pushing," says Alfred.

"Why?" asks Sonny.

"'Cause you got the goods to be champ."

"Of this?" Sonny jerks a thumb out at the arena, a gray cinder-block box that looks ready to crumble into the pitted black tarmac of the parking lot. Old fishing boats, paint peeling, masts cracked, bob in the harbor. We're in some coast town I've never heard of. I make a mental note to get the correct spelling of the town's name. For my book. Especially if this is where it all ends. What a pissant place to close down the story. But fitting. Ironical. And then I feel ashamed— I'm thinking about my book. This is Sonny's life.

3

After a while, Alfred asks, "What else you gonna do?"

"You mean what else YOU gonna do," snaps Sonny.

"I got my pension," says Alfred. "I can watch you play Indian for the tourists, sell your momma's made-in-China tomahawks."

In the rearview, I see Jake's wrinkled old face twist into a scowl. Sonny's mom is his niece, but he hates what she's doing more than anyone.

"Can't be worse than this," says Sonny. "Time to hang it up. It's never gonna get any better."

"Warriors welcome their fears," says Jake. "The Creator gives them fear to make their senses sharp."

"Not about being afraid," says Sonny. "About wasting time. For nothing."

"Let the Hawk find the way," says Jake.

"Later on the redskin crap," says Sonny.

"Let's just get on with it," says Alfred, "and then we'll all sit down and figure out what's next. Promoter booked us into a nice motel with free movies. Let's win the fight, relax, and tomorrow we'll have a big breakfast and

4

make some plans."

"You been saying that for two years," says Sonny.

Alfred opens the window and spits out the brown shreds. "What do you say, Martin?"

"Nobody's been punching at me," I say. I keep my eyes on the road, but I can imagine Sonny's sidelong glance. I know how to get his attention. "I'm not going to tell Sonny what to do."

It's sly but it works. You can't order Sonny around, even if you're right, but if you are, he'll come around. You just have to cut him slack.

"Don't count on me making any more plans after tonight," grumbles Sonny.

Back in the rearview, Alfred and Jake roll their eyes in relief. I let the air out slowly, through my nose.

We have to lift Alfred's wheelchair up the front steps of the arena. It's hard on someone who used to be a tough cop to be dependent, but for once Alfred says nothing. One wrong word and Sonny blows. Never seen this weird-ness before.

The arena is cold and shabby, wooden planks over the hockey ice and a crummy old ring. The ancient canvas is stained with dinosaur blood. The ropes are frayed, sagging. The ring is surrounded by folding chairs, another bad sign. Crowd doesn't like a decision, those chairs fly.

The promoter is waiting for us in his office. Typical small-town boxing sleazebag, cheap toupee and gold chains. "Tickets just ain't moving. Times are bad. The new TV shows. You know how they hate Indians around here. I didn't want to cut your percentage, so I moved you to a cheaper motel."

I think, No movies, but I say, "What about the marquee? Sonny's name was supposed to be first, and in bigger letters."

"Hadda do it for TV. They're shooting a documentary on Iron Pete."

"Why him?" growls Alfred.

"Who knows? Something about ethnic boxers."

"What do you think Sonny is?" I say. "Native Americans are the original ethnics."

"You talk to them, kid. I got my own problems."

The dressing room is chilly, damp. Rusted hooks in crumbly concrete. No hangers, no

6

lockers. The toilets haven't been flushed in weeks. No hot water. All the other fighters except Iron Pete, the local hero, dress in the same room with us. They're mostly white guys with dumb tattoos, eagles and skulls, skinny kids who washed out of the Marines or fat truck drivers who don't have good-enough personalities to be bouncers. They're getting their hands taped by their older cousins, fatter truck drivers with cigarettes dripping ash. Everybody gawks at us, two black guys, one in a wheelchair, an old Indian and a mixed-blood fighter.

"Someday, Sonny," says Alfred, packing extra gauze over the bad knuckle, "believe it or not, you gonna miss this, you'll be the champ and . . ."

Sonny's head comes up, his black eyes hot. "You'll say anything to . . ."

". . . you'll say, 'Life was simpler back then.'" Alfred winds tape over the gauze, across the fingers, down the hand, around the wrist. It's amazing how many times he does it, and he never takes shortcuts. He does it slowly and carefully every time. "Let's warm up." He puts a mitt on each hand. Sonny jabs at the right mitt

7

as Alfred moves it from side to side, then starts mixing up his punches, straight rights, uppercuts. He throws his money punch, the left hook. It looks slow, a rusty gate. He's not even working up much of a sweat.

"C'mon, c'mon," says Alfred. He follows Sonny's glance toward the door. "Who's that?"

"Hi there." She's wearing jeans and a safari jacket. Tall, slim, dark hair. She's only a few years older than Sonny and I, maybe twenty-three, but she's pretty sure of herself. "Sonny Bear?"

"No ladies in the dressing room," says Alfred.

"Wrong." She makes the word reverberate. "We won that battle years ago." She waves at the door. "Let's go, guys."

A man and another woman begin dragging in equipment.

"What's this?" asks Alfred.

"Just a few quick questions, we—"

"After the fight," says Alfred.

Her body tenses. "That means overtime for my crew. This is public television. . . ."

"This is private enterprise." My best growl. "Who are you?"

8

"I'm the third second." I realize how dumb that sounds, so I add, "And Sonny Bear's writer."

She lifts her thick black eyebrows into arches over her big brown eyes. I'm hypnotized. Then she says, "You must be joking." Acid drips off every word. I want to splash her with the spit bucket.

"An old trick," says Jake, throwing a robe over Sonny's sweaty shoulders. "Give him a chill, try to make his muscles stiffen up."

"You paranoid?" she asks. "We're just—"

"You're the ones changed the marquee on us," I say. "Who knows what else you're up to. You want your guy to win for your lousy TV show. Better clear out."

She ignores me and smiles at Sonny. It softens her face. Parts of my body perk up. "I'd really like you to be part of this film, Mr. Bear, good publicity and . . ."

"Out," snarls Alfred in his old bull-cop voice.

She looks cranked to argue, but the camerawoman grabs her arm and pulls her out of the room.

"Jab," orders Jake. "Listen to Alfred."

"I hear Viera is a banger, just keeps

coming," says Alfred, moving the mitts around. "He's made to order for you. Box him in the early rounds."

Bells start ringing. Whenever the door opens, crowd noise splashes in. The skinny kids and the truck drivers strut out for their matches and stagger back. One of them has to be carried. We stay in our corner and concentrate on moving Sonny around, keeping his muscles warm. Alfred makes him jog in place and throw combinations. Jake smears Vaseline on his face. I rub his shoulders.

"Viera butts," says Alfred. "Don't let him close. Push his head away."

Finally, the door bangs open for us.

"BEAR!"

2

THE ARENA IS PACKED; every folding chair has a fat white butt on it with a loudmouth on top. "Injuns!" someone screams, and there's an *F Troop* Indian war whoop and someone else gets up and dances in the aisle. The crackers call it comedy. Sonny ignores them.

The TV camera is set up near Iron Pete Viera's corner. The woman directs her crew like it's a major motion picture.

Iron Pete is a steroid yahoo with a ponytail almost as long as Sonny's, and a tattoo on his arm of an eagle gripping a sailboat in its talons. When he flexes his arm at the crowd, they start chanting "I-un PETE, I-un PETE."

I say to Alfred, "Sonny's going to have to drive a stake through his heart just to get a decision."

"Shut up," says Alfred.

I never pay attention to the introductions. This is when I recheck the ice bucket with our

11

taped water bottle, our sponges, the spit bucket. I steady the wheelchair as Alfred hauls himself out and finds a handhold on the ring apron so he can see the action and shout instructions between rounds. I don't know how he manages to hold himself up through a long fight.

Iron Pete comes right out at the bell, misses with a long, loopy right, takes two jabs and then clinches. He's six feet tall, an inch shorter than Sonny, but he's wider and heavier. While he's holding on he tries to drive the top of his head into Sonny's eyes. Sonny twists his body the way Alfred and Jake taught him and rams his shoulder into Iron Pete's nose. There are tears in Pete's eyes and he breaks the clinch.

It's a dull first round. Iron Pete shows off his two moves, a head butt and an uppercut to the groin, and Sonny can keep away from those in his sleep. Which is his problem. He's fighting like he's asleep. No fire, no energy. He's flat. He's going through the motions.

"Wake up—stick and move," Alfred screams, but Sonny is on automatic pilot, keeping Viera at arm's length, at the end of long, slow punches.

Between rounds, I sponge Sonny's neck and face, rinse his mouthpiece and tilt the water bottle up to his face. He spits some of the water out on me. Jake and Alfred are yelling at him to wake up, move, take the fight to Viera.

The second round he throws a few jabs, but mostly brushes Viera's punches aside. He doesn't seem to care.

At the bell, Alfred yells at me, "Throw some ice in his cup." When Sonny plops down on the stool I get ready.

Jake rubs his shoulders. "Move your head after you punch, Sonny. You forget everything?"

Just before the bell for the third round, I scoop out a handful of ice, pull out the waistband of Sonny's trunks and dump it under the leather belt of his protective cup. When the ice hits his crotch, he jumps up bellowing. It's my tail he wants, but Viera is roaring across the ring at him.

They meet in the middle slugging. It's one mad minute. They stand toe-to-toe and whale. Viera is strong, he can take it, but Sonny is driving him into the deck, *crack*, a jab breaks

Viera's nose, a left hook to the body crushes his liver, this is going to end soon. Sonny hooks over the jab, then throws a right. He's setting up Viera for a left hook to the cheekbone that will send us home early.

The right connects, and Viera's head snaps into the pathway of the hook to come. But Sonny never throws it. His face twists in pain. The middle right knuckle.

Viera takes advantage of that instant and throws an uppercut into Sonny's cup. I can imagine the ice crunching, driving up into his groin. Sonny leans forward and Viera brings his head up into Sonny's left eye. *Thunk*. Sonny staggers backward. The skin over his eyebrow opens like a red mouth. Blood sluices down over his eye.

We're yelling at the referee to call the butt. The camera crew is circling the ring to get more blood, and Viera is closing in, but Sonny knows how to move and spin and tie Viera up, and he manages to survive the round and get back to the stool.

Jake moves fast, pinching the cut with his fingers to stop the bleeding, then fingering in the ointment. I'm sponging like crazy, rinsing

14

and pouring. Alfred has pulled his way up on the ropes and is talking right into Sonny's ear: "Jab with the right, just to push him back. When he drops his shoulder to throw the uppercut, hook to the head."

The crowd is screaming for Viera to go for the eye and he tries, but Sonny is awake now, survival time, throwing out the right as if he's swatting flies, but Viera doesn't know it's useless, he's circling left, waiting for an opening. It comes soon. Viera bulls in, drops his shoulder to throw another uppercut to the groin, and Sonny lands a left hook to the iron head. Viera stumbles backward.

Sonny jabs, on him now, another hook drives Viera against the ropes. Two good hands and the fight is over, but Sonny has to get too close for a short punch like the hook. Viera lunges and scrapes the left eyebrow with the laces of his glove. It opens the cut.

"Take him out, now," Alfred is screaming, and Sonny surges forward, he's got Viera on the ropes, pounding him with his left, ignoring the blood and white stuff oozing over his eye and down his face. He's going to win, he's going to win!

But suddenly, an instant before Iron Pete gets smelted, the referee plunges between them and waves off the fight. He points to Sonny's bloody eyebrow. He holds up Viera's arm. If he didn't, Viera would fall down.

And that's it. A technical knockout for Viera. TKO. I'd score it a TRO, a technical rip-off.

Jake is screaming and Alfred is screaming, and a voice that sounds a lot like mine is screaming, but Sonny just shrugs and walks back to his corner, his shoulders slumped.

It's over.

Maybe it's all over. Seventeen fights in two years, win thirteen, lose four, every loss a hometown heist. That's no record for a future champion of the world. It's the record of an "opponent," a nobody who's good enough to put up a decent fight but not good enough to win the big ones.

The crowd is chanting, "I-un PETE, I-un PETE," as Viera dances around the ring flexing the eagle's wings. Sonny vaults the ropes and rushes off to the dressing room. We scramble to get Alfred back into the chair. Usually we have to clear a path for Sonny through the crowd. But this time no one bothers him. Sonny's invisible.

Maybe that's the last bad sign.

Hang it up.

T HERE'S A CAR WRECK and a stabbing ahead of us, so we sit in the emergency room for an hour before a nurse takes a close look at Sonny's eyebrow. She shrugs, makes a mark on her clipboard and walks away.

"So this is where it ends, in an all-night blood hole in a dead-end town." I don't realize I'm saying it out loud while I tap it into the laptop.

"Write it down if you have to," says Alfred, "but shut up."

"Leave him alone," says Sonny.

Alfred wheels around. *"Now* you want to fight?"

"He did the best he could," I say.

"I hope not," says Alfred.

"Don't matter now," says Sonny.

"Hi there. You okay?" The TV producer marches in and leans over to peer at Sonny's eye. "You were jobbed out there. I hope we

18

weren't part of the problem."

"'S okay," says Jake. "He's a professional."

"Was," says Sonny.

She gets it right away. "You're not going to quit?"

"Announce my retirement on your show."

"The way you were fighting tonight, you might as well quit," she says. "You started too slow. You didn't bring the fight to him until it was too late."

"What makes you think you know so much?" I ask, trying to get some sneer into my voice to hide the tremble.

"I'm a producer. I know everything." Her smile makes my liver quiver. "The deck was stacked. You had to knock Pete out to win. Ever since the fishing rights case around here, the locals've had it in for Native Americans. Think they had something to do with closing down their factory."

"Always be something," says Jake. "Got to overcome it. Learn from it."

"Sonny learned how to fight one-handed tonight," she said. "What happened to the right? Broken?"

"Don't want that in your movie," says Alfred.

19

"Hey, I'm easy." She smiles. "I might like to shoot your next fight." As the desk nurse passes us again she calls out, "You know, we have a hurt person here."

"Everybody in here's hurt, honey," says the nurse, popping out her words as if she's snapping gum.

"But not everybody comes in with the media." She flips open her wallet and shows the nurse a card. "Would you call your supervisor please, before I call my camera crew?"

The nurse scowls at her and marches away, but a doctor shows up a few minutes later. "Yes? Sonny Bear?" he says to her.

"I'm Robin Bell, Doctor . . ."

"Dr. Gupte."

"And this is Sonny Bear." She grabs Dr. Gupte's sleeve and tugs him over to Sonny. "He's a professional boxer, he will be on television, and we're concerned about septic conditions in his eyebrow. The skin needs to be debrided right away, and we have to have small, tight stitches, not much lip. Can you do that?"

"Of course. Please come this way."

Alfred winks at Jake, who shakes his head.

We follow Sonny and Robin back to the examination room.

Dr. Gupte and a nurse clean out Sonny's eyebrow, but when the sewing needle appears I'm out of there. I'm leaning against a wall outside the room, taking deep, queasy breaths, when I hear, "You, too?"

She's leaning against the other wall. The skin of her thin face is very white, a sharp contrast to her black hair and to the sprinkle of freckles over her nose. She looks younger, nicer.

"I can't stand the sight of blood," I admit.

"That's tough for a fighter's writer."

"The sight of Sonny's blood, really. There hasn't been a lot of it. He's good, not like tonight."

"What happened? Why'd he start so flat, as if he didn't care?"

I don't want to get into that, so I ask, "What's your film about?" These TV types love to talk about their projects, especially if you call them films, which makes them feel like Martin Scorsese.

"Well, it's about boxing, of course, but it's also about small-town America and ethnic pride and tribalism and the rites of manhood. . . ."

"Sounds like you haven't figured it out yet," I say. "I guess if you shoot enough, something'll develop."

Her face gets darker as the blood comes back. Not so nice, but more interesting. "What exactly do you write," she asks, "ransom notes?"

"That's cute." I decide there's no point being enemies. "It was supposed to be a book about Sonny becoming the youngest heavy-weight champion in history. Two years on the title trail. But we're sort of running out of time. He's nineteen years old; he'll be twenty in January."

"Who's your publisher?"

"Don't have one yet."

"Has anyone seen any pages?"

"I have to turn in the first few chapters next week to my new advisor."

Her eyebrows arch. "You're in college?"

"I'm trying to get an independent-study semester to finish the book."

She looks interested. Her eyes flick over me, leaving warm trails. "Where do you go to school?"

Just then Alfred rolls out with Jake. Sonny is giving Dr. Gupte and the nurse his auto-graph. Robin hurries over to be with the star of the show.

4

WE TRAIL ROBIN'S OLD BMW to an all-night diner just far enough out of town so that we get some strange looks, but nobody hassles us. We settle around a table.

"So what's the story with you guys? Where are you . . ."

"Old story," says Sonny. "Skip it."

"No, I'd like to hear it."

Sonny grunts, stands up and stalks to the video games in the front of the diner.

"All you need to know," I say, "is that Elston Hubbard is fighting in Las Vegas in two weeks, and if he wins, he'll get a shot at the title."

"I know that, I read the papers. So what?"

"Two years ago, Sonny was supposed to fight Hubbard for the Gotham Gloves championship. He would have beaten him, but he was declared ineligible."

"Drugs?" She's making notes, which annoys me. It's my story.

24

"No. He fought some smokers—they're like pro fights, only . . ."

"I know what smokers are," says Robin, annoyed.

"They found out about them at the last minute and disqualified Sonny because he wasn't an amateur. Hubbard went on to win the Olympic gold medal and here we are, picking up meatball fights in nowhere towns."

I suddenly realize I'm doing all the talking. Jake's eyes are closed; he could be sleeping, he could be going into the Moscondaga "little death," he might just be resting his eyes. Alfred has wheeled off to the bathroom. He'll be gone for a while. After a long, tough day the tubes and plastic bags that catch his wastes could be backed up, or at least tangled.

"You're kind of an interesting group," says Robin. Her pen is poised over her notebook. "How'd all you guys get together?"

"That's another book," I say. I notice that one of Jake's eyes is open a crack. "Ask Jake— it goes way back." His eye shuts.

The waitress bustles up. I can do this order in my sleep: deluxe burgers for me and Sonny, sausage and eggs for Jake, dry toast and tea for

Alfred. Win or lose, always the same food after a fight. Robin orders yogurt and coffee.

Sonny stomps back. "Got any quarters? Don't even have a bill changer here."

"All the quarters you need in Vegas," says Robin.

Alfred wheels back. "What am I missing?"

"You should go to Las Vegas and make Hubbard fight you."

Jake's eyes open.

Sonny snorts. "What kind of TV shows you make? Fantasy?"

"That's what Muhammad Ali did," says Robin. "Made so much noise they had to fight him. It's all publicity and connections."

"Just what we don't have," says Alfred.

"You've got to make your own publicity and connections. Marty's got a big mouth."

Sonny looks at her as if she's crazy and Alfred rolls his eyes, but Jake says, "Keep talking."

"Well, what's Sonny's big selling point? What makes him different from every other wanna-be champ?"

"The Indian card doesn't always play," I say. "You media types may love Indians, but out in the boonies . . ."

"We're talking big-time media now, New York, L.A. Stories in *USA Today*, on CNN, then the *Times* and the networks." Her dark eyes were snapping. "They're all out there in Vegas looking for things to write about. The champ is boring, Hubbard's a lox, and after you've seen John L. Solomon do his Yiddish shtick, it's over. They'd love a real live native warrior."

The food comes and I say, "So what do we do, ride out to Vegas on our pinto ponies and threaten to scalp Hubbard if he won't fight us?"

"I'm serious," she says.

"So are we," I say. "You may think this is kind of cute, hustling Sonny like a lounge act, but he's no sidewalk Indian, he's got the blood of the Running Braves. . . ."

Sonny drops into his seat. "C'mon, not you, too."

"Running Braves?" The eyebrows almost touch her hairline. "What's Running Braves?"

"Forget that," says Alfred. "You got a plan?"

"Not really, I just think you guys have to go out there and make things happen. Put yourselves into play." When the food comes, Robin grabs the check. "When you're champ, you'll owe me."

"Don't save your appetite," says Sonny.

"If you get off your butt, you'll make it," she says. "Because in your heart you really want it." She bores right into Sonny with those dark eyes. "You've got the killer instinct, Sonny, and what looks like a helluva left hook. You fought hurt and you would've put him away, without a right hand, without a left eye, you still would've won, if the referee hadn't stopped it to save him. If you can do that, you can do anything you want."

Nobody is breathing at the table. Alfred and Jake look at each other, then at her. Sonny glares right back at her. "How come you think you know so much?"

"My grandfather was a fighter, and I used to go to the fights with my dad, watched a lot on TV." She looks at her watch. "Gotta push." She gives each of us one of her cards. "Let's stay in touch. Don't sign any exclusive TV documentary deals till you check with me."

We watch her march out of the diner, her boots pounding a drumbeat.

"Vegas," says Sonny. He laughs the nasty little defensive laugh he uses like a jab to keep people off balance when he isn't sure what's going on. He looks at Jake. "Maybe the

Hawk'll fly me to Vegas."

"Maybe so," says Jake. "You got to listen to women. The Creator gave them special sight."

"She didn't look like a Clan Mother to me," I say.

Jake's eyes narrow. "Don't get in the way, Martin."

"Let's go." Sonny stands up.

"I'm not done yet," says Alfred.

"Wake up," says Sonny. "We are done and gone."

5

PROFESSOR MARKS WAVED the four chapters I had faxed him. "Witherspoon does Hemingway."

"You liked it?"

"Hated it." He threw my pages across his little office. They hit the wall and cascaded to the floor like a waterfall. Paperfall?

I sucked air. It was like taking an uppercut to the cup from Iron Pete.

"You're writing dead white male."

I mumbled, "At least I got one out of three."

"Sit down, Mr. Witherspoon. Grab yourself. We need to talk."

I dropped into a broken old armchair. I made fists but put them between my thighs. I couldn't decide if I wanted to throw him through the window or cry. I could do both.

"Mr. Witherspoon, what you wrote was not the voice of a nineteen-year-old urban Black male."

I wanted to say, "How you know, home-boy?" but I couldn't get anything up past the Styrofoam cookie in my throat.

"The information in your story is excellent. It reeks with the credibility . . ."

"I was there!"

". . . of journalism. This is not a course in journalism. You are applying for an independent study for creative writing. Creative writing! This is destructive writing. Who is Sonny Bear?"

"He's a nineteen-year-old half-Moscondaga, half-white . . ."

"Stop right there. I can read the sports pages. I can rent the Rocky movies. Why should we care about him? Why are you with him? What does it all mean? I need more from you. I hope you've got more to give."

The phone rang. He gave me a meaningful glance that was supposed to nail me to the chair, and he picked up the phone. "Bob Marks . . . Hey, Theron, how are ya? . . . Now that's good news. . . . What are the numbers? . . ."

He got into a heavy-duty money discussion and I checked him out. Medium-sized white guy, close to my father's age, mid-fifties, balding, pot belly, wearing zipper jeans, no-name scuffy sneakers, and a blue work shirt. Drab cool. I knew he'd written some novels and screenplays but I couldn't remember any of them. There was some reason he came here to be writer-in-residence but I had forgotten it. Maybe he was dying or a plagiarist or just losing it. Dying would be okay. I hated him very much.

He hung up the phone. "My agent. Sorry. Okay. Why should I care about Sonny Bear?"

"He's an interesting character struggling to find his identity, to find the world he belongs in."

"So what? I've heard that before. From Native-American writers who tell it better." He peered at me over his half glasses. "What do you, an African American raised in the post-literate hip-hop era, have to say about this?"

I took a deep breath. Trying to get permission for a semester of independent study was harder than trying to get into college in the first place. Grown-ups hate to set you free. I had to give them samples of my writing and beg two deans and three professors. I thought I had it nailed. I felt it all crumbling around me.

I sucked it up, then threw my best punch. "I

hope, Professor Marks, you're not saying that because I'm Black I can only write about the Black *thang.*"

He honked at me, that nose laugh some whites have. I hate it. "Don't try to mau-mau me, Witherspoon, I'm no Ivy League tenure hack hanging in for his pension. I'm a pro writer, a wordslinger between books and marriages, and I'm here to goose up the program and then ride into the sunset before anyone can shoot back."

What a pompous jerk. But all I said was, "My project has already been approved."

"By someone who is no longer with the university. I don't think this is a proper independent-study project. Or maybe you're not doing it right. Either way it doesn't work for me. It's got no heart, no grit. You love Sonny Bear? You believe in his quest? It reads like you're just along for the ride.

"Does boxing stink? Who's this guy in a wheelchair? I don't get a sense of Jake. This foxy TV producer, Robin Bell—sounds like a phony name to me. Does she make you jealous? Do you think she'll get between you and Sonny?"

"What's that got to do with the story?"

"That is the story. Otherwise, who cares, another guy wants to be heavyweight champ, so what? I want to be heavyweight champ, we all do, but most of us quit. He will too, probably. So will you. I liked when you thought about your book before you thought about Sonny. That was real."

The phone rang again. I thought about just walking out. It was green outside his window. I'd never been here in the summer before. It was hot in his office. Small office for a tiny talent. Books everywhere. Some had his name on them. *Queen Bea. The Runaround. Bronze Cannon Wrecks.* Never heard of any of them. Pudgy little opponent writer, had to get a college job because his books don't sell.

He finished his phone call. "If you want to borrow any of them, feel free."

"Thanks. I'll wait for the TV movie."

He smiled. Yellow teeth. "Now that's good, that's grit. Sarcasm works. Okay. First thing, you keep dropping these Indian tidbits along the way. What's the 'little death'? Who are the 'Running Braves'? What's 'the Hawk' mean?"

"I thought I'd deal with that later. Those were teasers."

"Foreshadowing. Okay. But they better pay off big-time. Now, let's talk style. First person is okay, I can live with that if it makes you comfortable, but then you've got to be more of a character yourself. Since you're filtering the action through your soul, we better know who you are. And if you're just playing writer, if you don't really care and you're not willing to let it hang out, it's going to show.

"Second major point, the present tense. It doesn't work. False immediacy, like you're writing one of those I'm-so-tough sports columns. You got to dig in, Witherspoon. Work harder. Maybe I'll sign your papers, but I want to see a few more chapters. Before I make a decision."

6

I JUMPED ON THE FIRST train back to New York. I was so pissed I was talking to myself out loud. This Professor Marks is a third-rater, an opponent who can't write the big one. He knows I've got a chance to be a contender so he's getting in my way. He doesn't want me to make it. And he's going to judge me.

Whoever I am. A postliterate rapper?

The little pink-faced conductor gave me his icy blue glare. No trouble on my train, boy. Who does *he* think I am, the president of the Crips? Professor thinks I'm not Black enough, the conductor thinks I'm too Black. I slipped on my ghetto stare and eyeballed him right back. It worked, even though my little round glasses slid down my nose.

I kept my hard face on until New Haven, when a posse of gang-banger wanna-bes pimp-rolled on and the conductor hid in another car. They looked at my clothes and my book bag, and one of them said, "Hungry?" and another said, "Fo' Oreos," but then they spied some honeys and forgot about me for the rest of the trip. I tried to read a book of experimental short stories that were written like movie treatments, but I couldn't concentrate. I kept thinking of things I should have said to Professor Marks. The friendliest was Drop dead.

New York City was hot and it stank, but I caught an air-conditioned subway car, and the ride uptown was icy sweet.

I stopped off at Donatelli's Gym on 125th Street in Harlem, my second home in the city. Just walking up those dark, narrow, twisting stairs calmed me down. The smell of sweat and liniment, the late-afternoon sun through the dusty windows, the bells, the scuffling footsteps of shadowboxers and the tom-tom slap of the speed bag cleared Marks out of my head.

Henry Johnson, who owns the gym, was working with a stiff who called himself the Punching Postman. I climbed up on the apron next to Henry, a formal man who always wears a white shirt and a tie. He's a good guy, one of Alfred's oldest friends. Henry has always let

Sonny train for free, doesn't even make him do chores around the gym anymore.

"Sonny around?" I asked him.

"They went back to the Reservation. He didn't even take his equipment. Said I could clean out his locker and give it to some other kid."

"You didn't do that?"

He shook his head but kept his eyes on the fighters sparring. "I seen this before."

"And what happened?"

He shrugged. "Sometimes they come back and sometimes they don't."

"You didn't try to talk to him?"

"No point. He's got to decide for himself. If he wants it bad enough, he'll come back."

"Cold."

He looked at me. "Got to be realistic in these situations, Martin. He's not getting anywhere. Money's not coming in. You got a fresh thought?"

"What about Robin Bell's scam?"

"Who?"

"The TV producer. About going to Vegas and challenging Hubbard."

"I heard that crazy talk."

"It worked for Ali."

"He already had big bread behind him. We're just small fry."

The Postman started getting hit, and Henry climbed into the ring to show him a move, which was a waste of time.

On the way out, I visited Rocky, the human-sized punching bag that hung from the ceiling by a thick chain. The dummy's canvas skin was divided into squares from forehead to waist, each marked with a number. The chin was 1, the right eye 7 . . . left eye 8, the nose 3 . . . middle of the belly 17. You get the idea.

I felt nostalgic about old Rocky. Three years ago, while I was in high school, my dad made me work out at the gym. I hated it. I felt out of place, and I was lousy at jumping rope and hitting the speed bag. I hated being there because I knew my dad, who once was a light heavyweight contender, thought I was a fat wimp wasting his life writing poems and short stories. I hated it even more when Henry paired me off with this wild-looking half-Indian kid Alfred had dumped on Henry after the kid got out of jail. We didn't get along at all. Each of us was supposed to take turns calling out the numbers while the other one hit Rocky. I did it in a flat monotone to show him I didn't care. And he wasn't trying too hard either.

And then one day, while we were at the bag, I heard a voice say, "Got to concentrate, Sonny. When a Running Brave chops wood, he thinks about the tree and the axe, not the fire he's gonna make."

It was Jake Stump, down from the Res to check on his grandnephew. He told Sonny to think about what he was hitting before he hit it, that a jaw was hard, a belly was soft. Then Jake whirled on me and fired a bony finger into my face. He said, "When you call a number, you gotta think, Why? Number nine, eye, so he can't see what's coming next. Number twenty-five, arm, deaden his muscle so he can't hit you so hard." Then he walked away.

After that, everything changed between Sonny and me, between me and my dad and even me and the world.

I took a few sentimental swings at Rocky. One thing hadn't changed. My best shot hardly budged the bag, and the pain in my knuckles shot up to my shoulder.

7

7

THE SUBWAY HOME was as hot and stinky and crowded as the streets. The apartment felt the same way. I guess I was depressed.

My kid sister, Denise, said, "Jake called."

I started for the phone, but she stopped me. "He said he'll call back. I don't think he wants Sonny to know he's talking to you."

Mom said, "It doesn't sound good."

"Sonny told Henry to clean out his locker and give his stuff away."

"Got to do something," said Denise.

"We offered some money," said Mom, "but we don't have enough to finance another year of this."

"It's not just money," I said. "Sonny's down. No publicity, no decent fights. He used the word futile."

Dad came in—you could hear his footsteps out in the hall. He's a super heavyweight now. I started to tell him about Sonny but he waved it

41

away. "What did your professor say?"

"Maybe that can wait for dinner," said Mom. She'll let you tell your story your own way.

Not Dad. "I like my news on an empty stomach. Well?"

"He wants some rewrites."

Dad nodded. "Well, writing is rewriting. You know that." Push comes to shove, Mom and Dad will always side with teachers against students, being teachers.

"It's not that—he wants something different. This white guy is telling me the book isn't Black enough."

Denise rolled her eyes and said, "Well, shut ma-uh mouth, if that cracker want some low-down niggerish licorish we'll . . ."

"Stop that," snapped Mom.

"Martin is a writer," said Denise. "He has to find his own voice. In his own time. In his own way."

Sometimes I can almost understand why most other people like that girl.

"Martin is a college student," said Dad. "He has to get his degree. Then he can go looking for his voice."

"You just don't get it," I said. "Some Hymie writer . . ."

"I don't want to hear that . . ." said Mom.

". . . who can't get his own stuff published . . ."

". . . garbage in my house. . . ."

". . . wants me to write some jigaboo rap fantasy."

WHAP! My dad's big hand shivered the table. "Stop this, Martin, right now. Some reality therapy. You are a student. Your job is to finish college. Then you can . . ."

"Maybe there's better uses for my tuition money."

That slowed the action. It's a sore point. My mother's mother, who owned a beauty products company, left me the money for college. It was in my name for tax purposes. I could get at it for anything I wanted, but I never have.

No telling where the conversation would have gone this time if the phone hadn't rung. Saved by the bell. Hey, Professor Marks, this is a boxing book, after all.

It was Jake. He wanted me to come up to the Res. Sonny was getting ready to leave.

8

THE RES LOOKED DIFFERENT to me every time. At first it was like a foreign country, every sight and sound exotic. I still have my notes from those first days, two years ago.

> . . . *back roads become green tunnels boring through forest into sudden clearing of dazzling sunlight . . . the Longhouse where the elders meet . . . the Stump, where any Moscondaga can call out the Nation . . . tangy smell of cooking sausage . . . woodsmoke curling out of chimneys . . . sun winks off hundreds of windshields in Jake's auto junkyard . . . sacred mountain Stonebird jabs into cloudless pale-blue sky . . . buffalo grazing . . . kid bangs lacrosse ball against family trailer . . . Alice Benton, Stump Clan Mother, ancient queen of wisdom. . . .*

I filled three audio cassettes with Jake's stories about how the Moscondaga fought in

44

every American war since the French and Indian, how they were cheated out of their lands and squashed into what was left of their reservation as the city of Sparta grew around them, and how the Nation lost its spirit.

Of all his stories, I liked best the ones about the Running Braves, a secret society of warrior-diplomats, always on call, always in training. A Running Brave could run a hundred miles, negotiate a hundred hours, fight to the finish, and speak with wisdom. The best of them could smell the breath of their prey a mile away and slow the beating of their hearts so an enemy would mistake them for dead. That was the "little death."

Jake's grandfather, Sonny's great-great-grandfather, was the last of the Braves. Supposedly he'd been killed by a hit-and-run driver while he was out on his daily run. But Jake said he was murdered by government agents who were afraid the Braves would liberate the Moscondaga from the corrupt chiefs who had sold them out. According to Jake, the government thought that they had finished off the Running Braves when they killed Jake's grandfather.

But Jake knew the secrets of the Running Braves, their training techniques and the way of the Hawk, the spirit that can lead a Brave to his destiny. He had taught Sonny. In the beginning, the stories sent chills up my spine.

But by the third and fourth trips, the stories got old and the Res looked like a raggedy slum of sagging cabins and rusted trailers. Jake's house was a shabby yellow box in a sea of rust and chrome. The Clan Mothers started to sound like nagging grandmas.

I decided that the Running Braves were just a redskin gang. Great-great-grandpa was probably a drunk run over by another drunk.

By then, I was noting all the empty beer cans and whiskey bottles along the shoulders of the rutted, dusty roads, and the scrawny dogs that never stopped yapping at the pickup trucks burning rubber. I couldn't stand the smell of those greasy sausages.

It was a while before I began to see the Res as a community, a poor neighborhood where the people were lighter-skinned than in my neighborhood and with a different accent.

Indians are just people. What a revelation, Professor Marks!

Jake picked me up at the bus station in Sparta. He didn't look good; since the Viera fight, his face had gotten puffy and his eyes were almost shut. When his diabetes and heart trouble kicked in together, he swelled up and lost the lightness in his step. He was glad to see me, but we didn't talk much on the drive in. You have to shout with the windows open in his noisy old pickup truck, and he didn't have the energy.

I noticed that some of the cabins had been painted and there were more TV satellite receivers around, and a few new cars I hadn't seen before. We passed a backhoe and cement mixer on the road.

"What you seeing?" On the Res, Jake was always teaching, testing.

There was a brand-new Mercedes Benz outside the log cabin of one of the subchiefs, Joe Decker, whose grandfather had been one of the chiefs who took the government side when it banned the Braves. Now Decker was smuggling cigarettes from Canada and selling them in Sparta. Jake and Decker had words one time, and the next day Decker drove past Jake's place a couple of times in an open jeep with an Uzi on his lap as a warning. I fired my finger at the Benz.

"I see that Decker and the cigarette gang got themselves a lucky strike."

Jake shook his head. "Bingo money."

"That's nickels and dimes."

"Not if you lease your land for a bingo hall."

"I don't understand. I thought the Nation voted against bingo."

"Council of Chiefs said no bingo on the Res, but some folks said it was their land, not the Nation's, they could do what they wanted." He jabbed a bony old finger down a road. I heard a bulldozer snarling. Dust drifted up over the trees. "Clearing land for a casino. Be poker, maybe slot machines."

"Can't the chiefs stop it?"

"Not without people get hurt. Decker and his crowd think they gonna get rich." He spat out the window. It was one way he punctuated sentences.

"Maybe they will," I said. "People got rich in Atlantic City and Vegas."

"Crooked white people. They'll come in here make Grandfather's Reservation into Godfather's Reservation."

I laughed. "Great line, mind if I use it?" I jotted it down.

"Joke for you, maybe." He clamped his mouth shut the rest of the way. When we pulled into his yard, his dogs scampered out, mean junkyard dogs, but once they recognized me they started whining to be rubbed. Especially the big white one called Custer. I always got a laugh out of his name.

Jake jabbed his thumb at the yellow house. "Up to you now. He won't talk to me. He's flyin' out in the morning."

9

SONNY WAS SPRAWLED in a reclining chair Jake had made from the bucket seat of a Volvo. There were empty beer cans around his boots. He didn't say anything when I walked in, didn't even look up, but that's the way he gets sometimes. I sat down near him. He was staring at two ESPN commentators blabbing about the heavyweight division. They said that everything was up for grabs, there hadn't been this much excitement since the days of Muhammad Ali.

"Got to get a piece of that action," I said.

Sonny didn't twitch. But I knew there was still a chance to get to him. He was waiting to be convinced, he hadn't made up his mind yet. The Indian part of him was going to listen to everything before he made a decision. That's how Indians are—they can sit in a Longhouse for days, listen to everyone, examine every possibility. Which doesn't mean they always make

50

the right decision. But there was a chance. Jake knew that when he asked me to come up.

One of the ESPN commentators said, "The pot of gold at the end of the heavyweight rainbow has even drawn an old champion out of retirement. John L. Solomon, who admits to being thirty-nine years old, thinks he has a chance against Elston Hubbard, Junior, the twenty-one-year-old favorite in the big-boy sweepstakes. Here the great John L. trains with sparring partner Sludge Wilson."

John L. Solomon looked pretty good for his age. He shuffled around the enormous gray-brown Sludge, popping punches at a shaved skull that resembled a mud bowling ball.

The picture dissolved into Solomon looking right into the camera and saying, "Sometimes kids need a *zetz* in the *tuchis*, as my Yiddishe momma used to say. That's why I'm coming back, first to spank Elston, then Floyd (The Wall) Hall, who is not worthy to wear the crown."

Elston Hubbard's father came on the screen. "Old John was a worthy champion in his time but his time ain't this time, which is the fine time of my boy, Elston, Junior."

Junior started sparring on the screen.

I said, "Alfred says Junior's dumb as a rock."

Sonny finally looked at me. "You came all the way to tell me that?"

"Yeah." The champion, Floyd (The Wall) Hall, appeared on screen and said something boring. "Floyd's not too swift either. He's the world's least colorful man of color."

"If it was brains, you could be champ," Sonny growled. I felt encouraged.

"You could whip any of these clowns."

"So get the match."

"You got to get it. You can't just sit here."

"Not gonna just sit here." He dug around the chair and brought up a fat envelope. He threw it to me.

The return address was for "Sweet Bear's Kiva," so I knew right away it was from his mom. I took my time poking through the twenty-dollar bills and the one-way ticket to Phoenix and a newspaper clipping about the opening of Sweet Bear's third Indian crafts boutique. They were all in the lobbies of fancy hotels managed by her new husband, Roger Russo. I'd never met either of them, but in the pictures they were a flashy couple. They'd made a ton of money with Indian crafts that Sonny's mom designed and then had manufactured in Singapore and Korea.

"You don't like Roger," I said.

"Don't have to live with them."

"Gonna work for them? Sell blankets?"

He sat up. "Don't want to talk about it." After a while, he said, "What are you gonna do?"

"Go back to school."

"What about your book?"

"You just knocked it out."

"Sorry." He actually sounded sorry, which made me feel bad, as if I'd purposely guilt-tripped him. Well, not all that bad.

"Doesn't matter. My professor doesn't like it anyway. Says I write like a white man."

"Which one?" asked Sonny. "Shakespeare?"

I laughed. "Wish I'd thought of that."

"Should of popped him."

"I wanted to."

Baseball players moved onto the screen, and Sonny started channel surfing until he clicked up MTV. A group called Dung Beetle was going nuts.

"Got some good fish for dinner," said Jake, shuffling in. "Gonna start cookin'. You boys go feed the dogs, close up the yard."

It was twilight. The cars and trucks in the junkyard were twisted animal shapes against the gray of Stonebird. Jake had always talked about Sonny doing his solo for three nights on the top of Stonebird, part of the ritual of a Running Brave. I pushed my luck.

"Can't leave—you haven't done your solo yet."

"Got to get out of this dump before it blows," said Sonny. "Gonna be big trouble behind this bingo."

"Be something for the Res if you fought for the title."

"Like they care. Decker told Jake last week he wanted only full-bloods living on the Res."

"Your mother's father was a chief."

He shrugged. We chased the dogs into the yard and closed the gates after them.

"What about Jake?" I asked.

"He can take care of himself."

After we fed the dogs and locked the gates, we washed up under the outdoor pump. It was dark now, and somehow not seeing him clearly made me feel closer to him, more confident.

"We're not done yet, Sonny. It's not over."

"It's over. Gave my stuff away."

"Henry's still got it."

He took some deep breaths before he said, "You been a real friend. Got to face it." His voice seemed small, faraway. Unsure? "We gave it our best shot."

"We blew it." I said it as harshly as I could. "We didn't go all the way."

"You think so?" He was unsure. I had him on the ropes. Did I have the killer instinct?

"Remember that TV producer?"

"The one you got the warms for?"

"C'mon, that skinny little . . ."

"Sure." He bumped me with his shoulder. "That old black owl head of yours did a three-sixty when she did that thing with her eyebrows."

"You noticed."

He laughed. "That girl was trouble."

"But smart. We could go to Vegas and do the Muhammad Ali number."

"Be serious."

"I am. You saw those guys on TV. It's all gimmicks."

"How would we get out there?" When I flapped my arms like wings, he asked, "How do we get the money?"

"You could cash your Phoenix ticket, and I got some money."

"You into mugging now?"

"Put away."

"School money?"

"Green money, what's it matter. . . ."

"Look at you, fat black boy with glasses. If you don't go to college, you'll starve to death."

"If it works, I could have a best-seller. Both be champs." Had to give him my best shot now, the money punch. My left hook.

"Look, Sonny, this is for me as much as it is for you. If I'm really your friend, let's just do it."

"You got a plan?"

Almost had him. "I'll figure it out on the way."

He gave me a shove. "Let's eat first."

Bingo.

10

THE WING DIPS, and I follow it down through the clouds toward a sea of neon.

"Wake up, Sonny." I shook his arm. He was already the world sleeping champion. "Vegas."

"Later." He burrowed deeper into the Moscondaga medicine pillow Jake made us take for luck.

"History, man. Your life."

"I'll read about it in your book."

"Here's the first line." I snapped open the laptop. I hadn't given up on the present tense yet. No matter what Professor Marks says, it pulls you right into the action. "'The wing dips, and I follow it down through the clouds toward a sea of neon.'"

"Sea of neon—I got to see this." Sonny grunted and leaned across me to squint through the airplane window. "Looks more like all the crayons in the world melted down."

"That's not bad." I tapped it in. "You write the first draft."

"You fight Hubbard." Sonny laughed and went back to sleep.

Wish I could. I never liked Junior Hubbard. The old man was a windbag, a better TV actor than he was a fighter, even though he had won the middleweight championship, but the kid was just a dumbo who got lucky. Ever since he won the Olympic gold medal that should have been Sonny's, he got ink and airtime he didn't deserve, not to mention the best training money could buy and a steady supply of opponents, punching bags with arms, to fatten his self-confidence and his record. Hubbard was sixteen wins, twelve by knockout, and nothing close to a defeat. All the experts said that once he got past old John L. he'd get a crack at the champ.

"Give it a rest," rumbled Sonny, closing the laptop on my fingers. Las Vegas rose to meet us, blinking like a crazy bloodshot eye. That was better than crayons, even better than sea of neon. You out there listening, Marks?

There were slot machines at the airport in Vegas, and they were getting plenty of action in the middle of the afternoon. We moved fast through the terminal, just carrying gym bags, traveling light and loose. I hated to spend the money, but we jumped in a taxi. Couldn't chance missing Elston Hubbard's workout and having to waste another day. Besides, I was starting to feel nasty, ready to rock. Didn't want to lose the Fever. Don't get it that often. This was my show.

The land was flat and scrubby, sandy desert washed in a shimmering yellow light I'd never seen before. Riding into town we passed a huge billboard with Hubbard's picture on it. I elbowed Sonny. "Should be you up there." I liked the gravelly sound of my voice.

The cabdriver said, "He's gonna win."

"How come?"

"Old John L. ain't hungry no more. Once Jews get rich, they lose heart."

"How you know I'm not Jewish?" I snapped.

He laughed.

"Sammy Davis, Jr., was Black and Jewish. So was Rod Carew, Major League Baseball Hall of Fame. The college professor and writer Julius Lester. Michael Jordan. So?"

He nearly drove off the road. "Michael Jordan?"

"How you think he made all that money?"

That shut him up for the rest of the trip. I didn't tip him. When we got out at the Garden of Eden Hotel, Sonny said, "Michael Jordan?"

"Made that one up. What does that redneck peckerwood honkie white trash cracker know?"

Sonny mimicked Jake. "That kind of talk don't get us anywhere."

"Got us here," I growled.

He squinted at me, as if he was seeing something new.

I liked that.

11

ONNY SHOULDERED through the hotel lobby and the gambling casino, and I followed close behind. I'd figured Vegas would be wall-to-wall Mafiosi in wraparound suits, and wildcat Texas oilmen blowing their salaries after months on a rig. But most people seemed to be family-plan tourists with tight shorts and camcorders. Packs of Asians. Old-lady robots sitting in front of the slots clutching paper cups of coins, waiting for the spinning pictures to *chunk-chunk-chunk* to a stop. Now and then the clatter of coins in the metal tray under the machine. Hard to imagine all this on the Moscondaga Reservation.

It took ten minutes to get to the nightclub where Junior was working out. More tourists in there plus boxing fans and reporters. Lots of red velvet and mirrors inlaid with golden designs. About as far from Donatelli's Gym as you could get. Made my juices hotter. All this so

Dumbo could spar and hit the heavy bag, and look how Sonny lives. Should have been the other way.

Sonny should be getting ready to fight John L. instead of standing in the corner, waiting for me to make my move. I felt a shiver of pure fear right down my spine. Cliché, pal, but that's where it was. Suck it up, Marty.

"Ladeez and gentlemens. Welcome to the camp of the next champ." Elston Hubbard, Senior, stood on the nightclub stage. He was wearing a white cowboy hat and nothing under his white leather vest but ropes of gold. He had a golden belt buckle as big as a paperback book on his white leather pants and white cowboy boots that looked as though they'd come off the belly of an endangered species. "The next heavyweight champion of the world, Elston Hubbard, Junior."

Hubbard came out onstage, jumping rope. The crowd cheered. He wasn't even that good a rope-jumper. Sonny was better.

"This is so sweet for me," said Senior, the mike almost in his mouth. "You mommas and daddies in the audience, you know what I'm feelin'." He crooned, "Myyyyyy boyyyyy."

Really tacky, but everybody was clapping or shooting their camcorders.

"To think this boy would grow up to be bigger and badder than his daddy. And just like his daddy he fought everyone on the way up. . . ."

Someone screamed, "EXCEPT SONNY BEAR," in an exceptionally loud and powerful voice. I was shocked to realize who it was.

People peeled away from me as if I was contagious. Even Sonny got a he's-not-with-me look on his face. Suddenly there was a clear path between me and Elston Hubbard, Senior.

"What's that, young man?"

"YOU HEARD ME. WHY YOU DUCKING SONNY BEAR?" By now every eye was on me. The fear was gone. My spine felt fine. Felt great.

"Elston Hubbard ducks no man," said Senior. "We'll fight 'em all. In turn."

"I SAY YOU'RE SCARED OF SONNY BEAR.

THE TOMAHAWK KID'LL SCALP YOUR HAIR."

Senior laughed, and said, "That boy's a poet, and he don't even know it."

The crowd applauded him. People were craning their necks to get a look at me. Shoot me with their cameras.

"MIGHT AS WELL BE FUNNY,

'CAUSE YOU'RE GONNA LOSE YOUR MONEY

WHEN JUNIOR GETS DECKED BY SONNY."

Now the crowd was applauding me. Even Junior laughed.

Senior kept the smile on his face, but you could see he wasn't enjoying it anymore. "Boy's read up on Muhammad Ali, a great champion and a great friend of me and Junior." He was smiling until one of the TV camera operators climbed up on the stage and nudged him out of the way so she could shoot down at me. He scowled. "Who you working for, boy?"

"SONNY BEAR. HE'S RIGHT HERE." When I pointed to Sonny, Senior's head jerked.

"Never heard of him." His eyes were cold.

"YOU CAN RUN, JUNIOR, BUT YOU CAN'T HIDE FROM SONNY BEAR."

The crowd was applauding me and pushing closer. Now they wanted to catch whatever I had. But Hubbard snapped his fingers and shouted, "Get him out of here—he's a spy from Solomon's camp."

A pair of serious gangsters started bearing

down on me. "Move it, boy," one of them said, pushing people out of his way and reaching for me, but then Sonny was shouting, "Back up," to the gangsters and one of them didn't and I shouted, "Watch your hands, Sonny," and he must have heard me because he didn't go for the face, which could have hurt him without gloves; he threw a half-speed left into the first gangster's stomach, which folded him over and sent him back into the second gangster. They went down like dominoes and took some camcorders with them.

There was screaming and shoving and we were surrounded by casino cops, linebackers with silvery guns who grabbed our arms and hustled us out through a back door and into the parking lot and threw us against a chain-link fence. Suddenly I was looking into the blinding sun. I was on my back on the asphalt.

A guy with a microphone blocked the sun. "So what's your name, pal?"

"Help me up, I . . ."

"Nahh, it's a better shot, you on the ground." He had a pile of silver hair. He put on a deep voice. "They say you're a spy for John L. Solomon, you've just been kicked out of Elston Hubbard's training camp, who ARE you and what's the story?"

"I'm nobody, but this is Sonny Bear," I said, pointing at Sonny, who was up and dusting himself off, "better known as the Tomahawk Kid, and we've come to Las Vegas to get the fight we deserve."

"CUT." The silver head turned. "You got it?" When the cameraman gave him a thumbs-up, he turned back down to me. "Nice bite, kid, that Tomahawk line's just what I need for the afternoon feed. That Daddy Hubbard spiel is getting old. How about we take the show over to John L.'s, see if we can make something happen for the overnight?"

12

JOHN L. SOLOMON worked out at the Oasis Hotel, at the other end of the Vegas strip. Once you got past the plastic sand dunes and the Kool-Aid waterfalls, the Oasis was just a low-rent version of the Garden of Eden. The lobby was tackier and the tourists were carrying Instamatics instead of camcorders. Drunks in cowboy clothes. The old ladies at the slot machines looked older and more desperate.

Solomon's training camp was as plain as Hubbard's was fancy, a huge gray basement room that smelled like an abandoned parking garage. Damp pipes snaked along the ceiling. A boxing ring was set in the middle of the room. That was Solomon's stage. No chairs. Hundreds of spectators crowded around the ring to watch Solomon make a big deal of his stretching exercises. We followed the TV guy into a section roped off for the press. Solomon was on his back in the middle of the ring, a fat little guy straddling him.

"I'm too old for this, Richie," moaned Solomon.

"That's what the Hubbards think, champ." Fat little Richie had a raspy voice out of an old white gangster movie. "Sit-ups, champ. Gotta pay for all those blintzes. One, two, oy, vay . . ."

The crowd laughed and clapped and John L. huffed and puffed through his sit-ups. He didn't look as good as he had on ESPN. He was big, at least six foot three, maybe 250 pounds, but a lot of it was around his middle. Hard fat but still fat. The skin of his chest and back was pale and freckly and covered with curly sandy hair. His head was balding. I remembered when his hair was fire-engine red and he was all over TV and on the covers of all the magazines. A white champion. He must have made zillions.

And now he was in a Vegas basement trying to make a comeback, the crowd grunting and groaning along with him. He'd stop to wink at people, and then Richie would pick up the pace and scold him and Solomon would wink some more and the crowd would cheer and Richie would pretend to get sore.

The TV guy whispered to me, "This stretching and kvetching routine is getting moldy. You guys ready to do your thing?"

"You mean just start yelling again?" I needed time to crank up to another nasty edge.

"Nah, I got that already. John L.'s pretty good—he'll play." He signaled to his crew. "Set up the monitor, cue the Hubbard tape."

We pushed closer to the ring. Solomon had a big, round face. The nose was mashed and there was a blue X scar on the bridge. His eyes were set deep under ridges of scar tissue. He took a lot of punches because he wasn't all that good, according to my dad, but he got a lot of press because he was a Jew from New York who wouldn't fight on Friday nights. He was only champ for about a year, and then for only one of the boxing associations. After he lost the title, there were hard luck stories, but I didn't pay much attention. Just another overrated white jock.

When he finished stretching, someone put on some Jewish dance music and Solomon started shadowboxing. I thought he was going to break into "Fiddler on the Roof," but he finally quit and came to the ring ropes, breathing hard.

The hairy sweater glistened. I didn't think he'd worked hard enough to be that sweaty.

"Dick. *Landsman*." Solomon reached down to shake the TV guy's hand.

"*Shalom*, Champ," said Dick. "I got some kids I want you to meet. They just gave the Hubbards some *tsuris*."

"Yeah?" Solomon looked at us and winked. He reached out and tapped me on the shoulder. "You must be the fighter. And ponytail's your record producer."

"You must be a comedian," snapped Sonny.

Solomon's eyes narrowed at that, but Dick shouted, "Look at this, John L.," and pointed toward his soundwoman who was holding up a TV monitor.

My face filled the screen yelling, "YOU CAN RUN, JUNIOR, BUT YOU CAN'T HIDE FROM SONNY BEAR." Hubbard was on screen, then mass confusion and me on my back in the parking lot.

"Love it," said Solomon. "Richie, get some gloves. Tape his hands."

The little trainer said, "You're not going to . . ."

"Nahh, we'll let Sludge check him out."

It happened fast. John L. pulled Sonny up into the ring and grabbed the mike. "Folks, a special treat this afternoon. Want you to meet . . ."

When he paused and turned to Sonny, I yelled, "Sonny Bear, the Tomahawk Kid."

"Sonny Boy, the Tomato Kid"—he began to laugh—"come to spar a round with Sludge Wilson, the strongest man in the ring today."

Sludge was even bigger than he looked on ESPN. He was bigger than John L., and less of it was fat. He was almost the same gray color as the basement. He could be one of the walls. He looked mean, bowling-ball head and pinprick eyes.

Sonny stripped off his shirt. He was wearing jeans and running shoes. I climbed up on the ring apron. "Stay away from him. Show your boxing. Stick and move, lots of combinations. Just don't let him hit you."

Sonny shook his head. "Won't mean anything 'less I stretch him out."

"He'll kill you." I was immediately sorry I said that.

"You can cash in my return ticket."

Sludge climbed up into the ring. It shook. He loomed over Sonny. John L. was winking away. Richie was shaking his head. The crowd stopped chattering.

"Sonny, look . . ." I tried to figure out what to say. I wanted to pull him out of there before he got hurt.

"My show now, Marty. Got to do as good as you did."

Richie stuffed a mouthguard in Sonny's face and pulled a leather guard over his head. Sludge waved away his mouthpiece and headguard. "Don't need it," he rumbled, and John L. led the crowd in applause. I always thought Sonny was big, but now he seemed small and vulnerable. If anything happened to him, it would be my fault.

"Now you happy?" Richie was standing next to me outside the ropes. He looked angry.

The only thing I could think of to say was, "The bigger they are, the harder they fall."

"You may think it's funny, but I'm trying to get John L. ready for the fight of his life. We don't need this."

"We do." I tried to sound as tough and raspy as Richie.

"You're a real mouth, you know that? Tomato Kid better have good insurance."

"His hands're his insurance, pal. Be surprised if old Slug lasts the round."

"Put your money where that fat mouth is," rasped Richie.

"Five hundred." All the cash we had. For our tickets home. I felt sick.

Richie grinned at me.

Sludge looked at Sonny the way Custer the dog looked at hamburger. There was foamy slaver in the corner of his gray lips.

"Don't kill 'im, Sludge," yelled Richie, "just cripple 'im," and Sludge grinned at the crowd with his pointy gray teeth, and then waved at Sonny to come on over the way a grown-up beckons to a toddler. The crowd laughed and popped their flashes. I was scared that Sonny would rise to that bait, the way I rose to the bet.

I yelled, "Stay away—dance him."

John L. himself rang the bell, and Sonny walked right out and hit Sludge with everything he had, a powerhouse left hook that would have killed a Cadillac. Sludge shook his head as if a fly had landed on his nose. Solomon laughed. Richie gave me an elbow in the ribs.

Sonny stood there trying to figure out what to do next when Sludge fired a right into his chest that knocked Sonny on his butt. Bang. Sonny got up slow, a red mark spreading on his chest.

"Whadya think," yelled Solomon to the crowd, "enough's enough?"

When the crowd started chanting "E-NOUGH, E-NOUGH," Solomon started climbing back through the ropes.

But Sonny was already charging Sludge.

"Move—stick and move," I yelled.

"Run for your life," yelled Richie.

Sonny took another hard shot to the body. It rocked him, but he stayed up and popped two quick jabs into Sludge's face. Sludge wrinkled his nose. The crowd laughed again.

They were whaling now, back and forth, throwing punches, in close, and then suddenly Sonny slipped a right; he just tilted his head so it whistled over his shoulder and he slammed a left hook into Sludge's liver. When the gray slab froze, Sonny stepped back, banged a right to Sludge's temple and slammed a hook into Sludge's jaw.

Sludge sank to his knees. The crowd roared—it had to be a joke. Sludge looked as though he was trying to pray, but couldn't quite get his gloves together. His brow wrinkled, and the skin continued to ripple up his bald head. His eyelids dropped like window shades. The laughter faded, grew nervous. Sludge pitched forward on his forehead. I heard Richie gasp. Sludge rolled over on one side. The ring shook.

I gave Richie the elbow. "Bigger they are . . ." but he was through the ropes, with smelling salts. John L. helped him roll Sludge over. It was a while before Sludge got up, real slow, blinking. Another trainer helped him down from the ring and out of the room.

Sonny watched from a neutral corner, his elbows hooked on the ring ropes, looking nonchalant and arrogant at the same time. Once our eyes met, neither of us could stop grinning.

John L. picked up the mike. "Now I see why the Hubbards didn't want this boy in their camp. He's dynamite. Well, I want this boy on my side. What do you folks think?"

The crowd cheered.

John L. pulled Sonny out into the middle of the ring and threw an arm around his shoulders. "He's gonna spar with me, and if he don't hurt me too bad"—he led the crowd in a big chuckle—"I might let him in on a few secrets.

Who knows, when I'm ready to give up the title again, I just might give it to Sonny Boy here."

"Bear," snapped Sonny. "Sonny Bear."

"See, he ain't even afraid of King Solomon. I like that." Suddenly he pointed at me. "You, come up here."

It took me a few seconds to understand. Richie goosed me with a water bottle, and I stumbled through the ropes and nearly fell down. John L. grabbed me in his other arm. "What's your name?"

I don't know why I changed my middle name on the spot, but I did. "Martin Malcolm Witherspoon."

Sonny looked at me.

"Martin Malcolm Witherspoon. You Sonny's manager, his trainer?"

"No, they're still in New York. I'm his . . ." I stopped before I said third second again. ". . . writer."

"Writer," bellowed John L., winking at everybody. "I like that. I'm from the People of the Book myself. It's ancient and it's modern. Sonny Boy's gonna need a writer. This here's the future, folks, my new protégé.

"Think of it, the fighter and his writer, the

people that Elston Hubbard, Junior, and that blowhard father of his are so afraid of, are here in the camp of the champ." He squeezed us. "*Mazel tov, boychiks*. We are going to make history."

13

SUDDENLY, WE HAD a room in the Oasis. It was a small room, two narrow beds and a single window overlooking the volcano that erupted every twenty minutes after twilight, but it was ours and it was free. We each had a card that entitled us to sign for all the food we could eat in the coffee shop off the lobby. Solomon's training camp would pay for it. We had T-shirts with caricatures of John L. and Richie sparring, and "OY, VAY" in cartoon balloons over their heads. We were on the team.

But Sonny was down. That night, back in the room after dinner, he sat on his bed and stared out at the volcano. Before it erupted, the volcano growled for thirty seconds. It was that distorted, over-amped noise you hear in movie theaters with wraparound sound. Then a geyser of steam shot up and an avalanche of plastic lava poured out as dopey music swelled and lights twinkled.

"Hot and smoking," I said, to cheer him up. "Just like us."

He grunted. The volcano's neon lights splashed against his face. The scar was a tiny railroad track over his left eyebrow. Dr. Gupte had done a good job—not much lip. "What did you think of Solomon?"

Sonny never asked questions like that unless he wanted to offer an opinion, so I played straight man. "What did you think?"

"A bull artist," he said. "Like Hubbard."

"They're trying to promote a fight."

"All that stuff, my boy, my protégé . . ."

"Maybe he likes you."

"In one minute?"

"Maybe he liked your coming out here on your own, talking your way . . ."

"That was you."

"I just made noise. You decked Sludge."

He sprawled backward on the bed. "All that Jew talk."

"He's Jewish. Maybe he's proud of it. Maybe he thinks it sells tickets. Who cares? What's bugging you?"

I'd forgotten that you can't always be direct with Sonny. He'll go away on you. He sat up and turned on the TV. He said, "You're a bull artist, too."

"I make promises, you deliver. That's why we're a great team."

He changed channels and the topic. "Think we should call Jake? Tell him where we are?"

That meant it was my job. Jocks are like that. If they ask if you're cold, it means they're cold and they want you to close the window and turn up the heat. It comes from having everything done for them. I dialed direct, but the hotel operator came on and said we couldn't make any long-distance calls from the room, even collect. Training camp rules. That made the whole deal seem more real. But I was too tired to go downstairs and call collect from the lobby. Sonny's eyes were closed; he was already snoring. I thought I'd just rest for a minute before I went downstairs. I tried to keep myself awake by trying to figure out what was on Sonny's mind. Why should he care what Solomon thought of him? We weren't here to win a popularity contest. Unless he didn't trust Solomon being nice to us. Except for Jake and Alfred and me, not too many people had really reached out to Sonny in his life. Most people are put off by his hard crust. It takes a while to see there's a good guy underneath.

Next thing, the phone rang. It was five A.M. I recognized Richie's rasp. "Drop your putz, klutz. Road work. In the parking lot in ten. Shake it." He hung up.

It took me almost ten minutes to get Sonny out of bed.

John L. was in the parking lot bouncing in his black combat boots. Under his Oasis sweatshirt, his gut was bouncing, too. He slapped Sonny on the back, and they took off with a couple of John L.'s sparring partners. I didn't see Sludge. A pink sun was streaking the gray sky. I got into the back of the chase car with Richie. He handed me a paper container of coffee. I got some down my throat and some on my pants, as the car followed the fighters down side streets and out toward the desert.

"Some piece of work you pulled off yesterday, kid. Don't let it go to your head."

"What do you mean?"

"This is the champ's big shot. If you guys mess it up, you're dead. I'm serious. Dead."

He looked serious.

"Mess up what?"

"Try to make him look bad. Hurt him. In any way."

"Why should we do that? He's the only chance for Sonny to get over."

"Just don't try to make it over John L. Get me?" His face was about an inch from mine. Every word felt like a sandstorm.

"Got you. So what about the five hundred dollars?"

"You'll get everything you deserve." He made it sound like a threat. He tapped the driver. "Get up closer, give 'em the horn, make 'em run faster." He turned back to me. "Bring Sonny downstairs at ten sharp. Just the two of you. Don't tell nobody."

After the run, which couldn't have lasted more than twenty minutes, we went back to the room and showered and put on the only clean clothes we had. At breakfast, I asked Sonny what he and John L. talked about on the run.

"He could barely breathe. If the fight goes more than a few rounds, he's in trouble."

Sonny went back upstairs to sleep. I read all the newspapers I could find. Every one had a story about Sonny Bear bursting into

Hubbard's camp, and every one had at least one mistake, little ones like spelling his name wrong, and big ones like declaring that Hubbard had paid us to do it for publicity. One writer called Sonny a "Muhammad Ali Wanna-Be" and a columnist from New York called him a Trojan horse, a trick by Hubbard to get a spy into Solomon's camp. Not one of the newspaper stories mentioned me, even though I was in most of the photographs.

I clipped every story for my file. Then I wandered around the hotel, looking in the shops at the jackets and hats and stuff we could afford once I got the five hundred dollars Richie owed me.

At nine thirty I woke Sonny up and started the process of dragging him down to the basement training camp. An armed guard blocked the door until Richie came out to get us. John L. was warming up in the ring. He was the only person in the room.

Richie whispered, "Work his body all you want, but no head shots, get it? And don't you guys ever mention this to nobody."

Richie started to tape Sonny's hands, quickly and efficiently, but not nearly as carefully as Alfred did. I said, "Middle right knuckle needs extra padding."

"So you do it," said Richie, dropping Sonny's hands.

"I never did it before."

"Smart-mouth boy like you knows everything," said Richie.

Sonny nodded. "You been watching everything, you can do it."

While I wound the gauze around Sonny's hands, Richie told him, "You're going to pretend you're Hubbard. Keep moving right, you're moving away from John L.'s right hand, his best punch, and you're dancing so he can't get set. He's gonna try to cut the ring on you and bull you into the ropes. You want to spin out, clinch when you need to, punish him with body shots. But don't touch his head. Get it?"

Solomon grinned at Sonny as he climbed into the ring. "Don't hold back, Sonny, I want you to try to knock me out."

I heard Richie mutter, "Over my dead body," before he rang the bell.

They sparred for five rounds, but I don't think any were standard three-minute rounds. If Sonny was spinning away from Solomon,

Richie might call "Time!" after two minutes. But if John L. had worked Sonny into a corner and was landing punches, he might let it go three and a half, even four minutes. He was trying to build up John L.'s confidence.

John L. was still strong, but his reflexes were gone. He was reacting in slow motion to Sonny's punches, and Sonny was throwing half speed. Meanwhile, it was as if Sonny had radar; he could spot one of John L.'s punches before it left the launching pad, pick it off in midair. If they fought for real, Sonny would win.

I tried to be diplomatic with Richie. "I guess John L. is sort of taking it easy on Sonny," I said.

He gave me a long, hard look. "Don't try to soap the soap man. All the champ's got left is heart and maybe enough tricks to keep Hubbard from hurting him too bad."

"Why are you letting him fight?"

"Ain't my idea, believe me. I don't even want to be here. But he needs somebody who cares about him."

14

ONNY AND JOHN L. ran together at dawn for ten days and sparred secretly every morning. John L. seemed to be getting sharper. In the early afternoons, they worked out in front of the crowd. You could tell they were getting to like each other.

John L. made a big deal of introducing "Sonny Boy, the Tomato Kid," and Sonny would growl, "Sonny Bear, the Tomahawk Kid," and John L. would wink at the crowd and say, "What's a Yid know from Indians?" and then they would take turns slamming the heavy bag and rattling the peanut bag, and doing calisthenics and jumping rope.

On the fourth day John L. suddenly turned to Sonny, palm out, and said, "How," and Sonny said, "Oy, vay," and we all cracked up. Sonny can surprise you that way—he can act like a dumb thug and then come up with something really smart. After that, they ran that bit every day, it was their little thing, and even raspy old Richie's eyes would twinkle.

"The kid's good for John L.," Richie told me one dawn in the car. "John L. hates to train. He gets bored real easy. I'm glad you guys showed up."

"Five hundred dollars glad?" I rasped.

"Don't push your luck, pencil boy."

Sonny never sparred with John L. for the crowd. An old sparring partner would go through the motions, never laying a glove on John L. After the public session was over, Richie would coach Sonny. He'd talk strategy. He'd put on the big mitts and review combinations.

I learned from watching Richie. He corrected some bad habits Sonny had fallen into, like dropping his shoulder so low before throwing a body hook that he left his face wide open. Sonny was a fast learner with lots of energy, and I could see that Richie enjoyed teaching him. He could forget about John L. for an hour or two. He made Sonny go outside after the coaching and run again for twenty minutes to get used to the heat.

My folks were excited when I called home;

they'd seen me on TV. My dad never asked where I got the money for my flight. Jake sounded happy, too. Alfred asked a lot of questions about Sonny's training. There was no way I could lie to him about the secret sessions with John L.

"Shouldn't need that kind of work so close to a fight," said Alfred. "Don't bet on Solomon."

John L. invited us to have dinner with him one night. He had his own cottage by the hotel's golf course—three bedrooms, a huge living room with a monster TV set, gold bathrooms. We ate outside on the patio overlooking the pool, with a dozen other people, family and friends and lawyers. John L. put us near him at the long table.

"So, what kind of Indian are you?" he asked.

"You never heard of it."

"Would if you told me. Be proud of your race, make your race proud of you."

"Moscondaga. Up near Sparta, New York."

"You don't look so Indian."

"My father was a white man."

"Was?"

Sonny got a funny look. "Died in Vietnam."

John L. leaned back in his chair and put his hands on top of his big gut. "My granpa Moise came over from Russia, settled in Brooklyn. Brighton Beach. That was like a reservation— you could walk on the boardwalk, hear nothing but Russian and Yiddish. English is my fourth language." He winked. "Third one was punching out anybody called me kike. Roots make you strong, Sonny Boy. And after I messed up . . ."

"Bad breaks can happen to anybody," said one of the lawyers.

". . . I had a place to crawl back to."

My mouth was full but I couldn't miss the chance. "How'd you mess up? The papers said . . ."

"Papers always get it wrong. I blew it, didn't train, let it all go to my head. Women, booze, dope." He winked. "Maybe I got my break too early. The world's upside down, once you can afford things, everybody gives you stuff for free."

"But you pay for it," said Richie.

"Jewboy, redskin, schvartze"—he winked at me—"same books, different covers."

He winked too much. I finally figured out he had a nervous tic. Did it have something to do with his brain? The reason Richie wouldn't let Sonny hit his head?

The next morning, in the car, Richie said, "You think Sonny be willing to fight the undercard?"

I thought he was teasing. "Nah, we're just out here for the sun."

"Worth two grand."

"You serious?"

"Sludge took off. He was supposed to fight one of Hubbard's sparring partners in a four-round prelim."

"Who?"

"A pretty decent banger, used to be ranked, but he got into drugs, now he's trying to make it back up. I don't think Sonny'll have any trouble with him."

I tried to stay cool. "He got a name?"

"Dave Reynolds."

"Dave the Fave?"

"You know him?"

"Yeah, he trains at the same gym Sonny does when he's in New York."

"So what do you think?"

"Sure, but Sonny's manager's in New York. Alfred Brooks. He should be here."

Richie nodded. "The champ likes you boys a lot. We can get the hotel to comp some more rooms, but you'll have to cover the plane flights. We can front the dough off your purse."

I fell back in the car, letting the coffee slop on my pants. Just like that, I'd made Sonny's big-time match. His breakthrough.

That morning John L. zigged when he should have zagged, and Sonny smacked him in the face. It wasn't a hard shot, a slow right cross, and John L. shook it off, but from the look on Richie's face you'd have thought Sonny dropped a lead pipe on John L.'s head. Something must really be wrong with Solomon.

John L. invited us to dinner again that night, but this time it was just the four of us. Sonny brought him the medicine pillow. You could see how pleased John L. was by the gift; he kept touching it.

He was very relaxed that night, talkative. "Tomahawk Kid—I like that. When I was starting out, I had a manager, dead now, called me the Maccabee Kid. You ever hear about the Maccabees?"

We didn't even get a chance to shake our heads.

"Tough Jews, the Maccabees. They whipped the Syrians—they were some kind of fighters." He was squeezing the pillow in his big freckly hands. "When Papa Maccabee died, the oldest boy, Judah, took over, and when he got killed, his brother Jonathan took over, and then Simon. I loved that story. I never had brothers. Would've liked that, a kid brother. A son." He was looking at Sonny. "I might have a son someday.

"You always hear about Jews being People of the Book, but we've always been fighters, had to be to survive. Like Indians. I mean, what's a ghetto, just an Italian word for reservation, right? Jewish kids grow up, they hear about the Holocaust, about getting knocked around, they should also hear about Benny Leonard, Barney Ross, all the great Jewish boxing champs. . . ."

"Relax, champ," said Richie, "don't get all . . ."

"Whatcha got if you don't got history, right, Sonny?"

Sonny surprised me. "Moscondaga once had a secret society of warriors, the Running Braves. They stood up to the government when it tried to wipe out our language, our culture. . . ."

"Same story. The Maccabees rose up when the Syrians wanted us to worship Greek gods." John L.'s face was bright red.

"You ought to call yourself something like that," said Richie. "Running Brave or Chief . . ."

"That's sacred stuff," said John L. "Be like me calling myself the Fighting Rabbi."

Richie rolled his eyes at me, but Sonny and John L. exchanged glances; they were really getting to understand each other. I felt good for Sonny, but a little cut out.

Richie arranged for us to borrow one of the white double-stretch limos the hotel used to pick up their big gamblers. It had a bar, a phone, a fax and a TV with a VCR. Sonny and I waited in the back while the driver met Jake and Alfred in the terminal. Their eyes bugged when they saw the limo. Sonny and I were laughing so hard we didn't see Robin until she climbed in.

"You?" I sputtered like a geek.

She gave me the eyebrows. "Hey, you wouldn't be here in the first place if I hadn't come up with the idea."

15

AT SIX O'CLOCK IN the evening it was still so hot in the parking lot outside the Oasis that it hurt to breathe. In the ring, under the TV lights and the canvas top, it must have been more than a hundred degrees. Richie knew what he was doing, making Sonny run in the heat. I hoped it would cool off before John L. fought.

There wasn't much of a crowd yet in the ringside seats where the stars and the high rollers would sit for free, but the portable stands that climbed into the sun were packed with real fight fans who wanted to get their money's worth and check out the Tomahawk Kid. He could be the future.

There was a burst of New York rap as Dave the Fave came barreling down the aisle, waving, blowing kisses as if he'd already won, then Alfred clearing the way for Jake and Richie, who had Sonny between them. I stood

95

up and caught Sonny's eye with a double-pump fist. He winked, which made me feel good. Or maybe he winked at Robin, who was standing on her chair next to mine. Or maybe he'd just caught John L.'s tic.

"He looks good," said Robin. The fighters were climbing into the ring.

"He hasn't done anything yet," I said.

"Just being up there is something."

"You must feel pretty proud of yourself," I said. It came out sort of twisted, and she lifted an eyebrow.

"It was all my idea, Marty, that's true, but ideas are nothing until someone makes them happen." She leaned over and kissed my cheek. It burned. "You did it."

I was embarrassed. "I just made noise. He did it." I changed the subject. "How come you're not shooting?"

"It costs thousands to get the rights to a fight. I'm grateful to get a free ticket."

The ring announcer was a young guy who seemed to be auditioning for the big time. He made it sound like a title fight.

"An important bout for two young fighters, and for those who want to see the stars of

96

tomorrow TONIGHT! In the black trunks, weighing two hundred and twenty-five pounds, from Harlem, New York, the crowd-pleasing rapper, Dave (The Fave) Reynolds."

Sonny stood still as The Fave wiggled and pranced around. Sonny didn't move as he was introduced.

"You've been reading about him lately, the Native-American slugger who came down from the hills of the Moscondaga Reservation in New York to win a place in John L. Solomon's training camp and in our hearts. In white trunks, weighing two hundred and ten pounds, the Tomahawk Kid, Sonny Bear."

The referee signaled them into the center of the ring to listen to him repeat the instructions he already had given them in the dressing room.

The Fave held out his gloves, Sonny reached out to tap them, and then The Fave pulled his gloves back and stuck out his tongue at Sonny. An in-your-face schoolyard put-down. He danced back to his corner, waving his arms over his head. Sometimes the brothers can be so stupid.

"Mistake," I said to Robin. "It's over."

If you blinked you missed the fight. Sonny

strolled out at the bell, loose and easy, no rush, and let Dave throw the first punch, a hard jab that glanced off Sonny's forehead and left The Fave wide open for the left hook that crushed his right cheekbone. He never saw it coming. Dave was moving forward behind his jab, just the way he was supposed to, his right hand cocked, and Sonny's punch stopped him cold and straightened him up.

Dave froze. His left arm was high and straight out, his right hand shoulder height, the statue of a boxer about to go down. Sonny took his time, a straight right that nailed The Fave shut, a second, unnecessary left hook that just glanced off Dave's head because he was already on his way out. The referee could have counted to one hundred.

Robin and I jumped up and down and hugged, which made my body hot and cold. I pulled away, but she didn't seem to react one way or another.

The dressing room swarmed with reporters and Vegas types trying to get close to Sonny. The TV crews circled him, the gray worms at the ends of their sound booms hovering over his head.

"Moscondaga—how do you spell that?" one reporter was asking Sonny.

"That last punch, was that a hook?"

"Isn't that the tribe having all those gambling problems?"

"I'm on a deadline, pal. You covering boxing or politics?"

After a while the mob broke into little discussion groups, Alfred describing how he first met Sonny in a drug bust in the Port Authority in New York, Jake talking about the Nation, Richie explaining how he and John L. had taught Sonny everything he knew. Sonny was going over the fight, nanosecond by nanosecond.

Suddenly, bodyguards started pushing people aside to make a path for Elston Hubbard, Senior.

"Eee-ficient work, young man, that was eee-ficient work." Senior swam like a big black shark through the crowd. "We need to have a talk."

"Talk to my manager," said Sonny, pointing to Alfred, wheeling up.

"Uh-huh," said Senior. "But does he have the a-bility to take you to the top of the mountain, the men-tality, not to mention the mo-bility?"

Alfred caught that last word, and his jaw clenched. I tried to think of something to say, but before I could, someone yelled, "It's John L.," and all the cameras swung around.

John L. Solomon, in the famous black robe he wore when he was starting out, the Star of David over his heart, MACCABEE KID on his back, was moving toward Sonny, his arms open. His hands were already taped.

"Never seen this before," one of the reporters whispered. "Right before his own fight."

"Beautiful, Sonny Boy. You made me proud as a papa. Make me want to go out and do the same thing."

They hugged. Could those be tears in Sonny's eyes? That would be an upset.

"You can do it, John L.," said Sonny. "Beat Hubbard and beat the champ, and then . . ."

"Then Sonny Boy gonna come after his papa," roared John L.

Everybody in the room laughed, but I looked at Sonny's face and I suddenly knew what Sonny was thinking about: our first night in Vegas, he was thinking about Junior and

100

Senior, his own dead father and John L., and then I thought, Now wouldn't that be something—John L. and Sonny fighting for the heavyweight championship of the world.

. What more could a writer want?

16

W E WATCHED THE MAIN event in John L.'s section with his family and friends. They pinched Sonny's cheeks and pulled his ponytail. He just laughed along with them. A different Sonny. He seemed relaxed, easy in his skin. The sun setting behind the Oasis cast a sweet pink light over his face. I'd forgotten how good-looking he was. Strangers stopped to introduce themselves, give him business cards, notes. One woman tried to give him her hotel room key.

"Gonna get worse," said Jake.

"Hope so," said Alfred. They laughed.

The ringside seats were swarming with women who would have worn more clothes in the pool and guys who were either actors playing gangsters or the real thing. Packed with jumpy, murmuring people, the parking lot was a theater-in-the-round now. The ring was the stage. It was still hot.

Elston Hubbard, wearing a blue silk jacket that had SENIOR in white letters on the back, led his son down the aisle. The kid had JUNIOR on his back, and all the handlers had HUB-BARD.

"You think Hubbard'll try to muscle in on Sonny?" I asked Alfred.

"Count on it."

"You worried?" asked Robin.

"If he can help Sonny more than I can . . ." Alfred shrugged.

There were endless introductions, athletes, actors, singers, comedians, and then the ring announcer, who looked like the father of the guy who'd announced Sonny's fight, said, "And now, someone you'll be seeing lots more of in the future—the sweat hasn't dried on his one-round kayo of Dave Reynolds—let me introduce to you the Fighting Chief from Moscaloosa, Sonny Bear."

"Moscaloosa." Robin made a face at Jake. "Chief."

"Don't matter," said Jake. "White men don't know and we don't care."

"White men," said Robin. "That lets Marty and me off the hook."

We laughed and shoved Sonny out into the aisle. He got a big hand. Standing under the lights, his hair still wet from the shower, in a fringed white shirt with pale-blue and orange beads, he already looked different. Bigger. Famous.

The heavyweight champion, Floyd (The Wall) Hall, was introduced. The booing died as he stomped around the ring shaking hands. He was taller and wider than anyone. He loomed over John L. and Sonny.

Muhammad Ali was introduced to a storm of applause. People stood. Ali was wearing a dark suit and red tie. He had trouble getting through the ring ropes. His face was a brown moon. He shook hands with Floyd and Junior and John L., and he whispered in Sonny's ear. We all looked at each other, feeling proud, as if the great Ali was whispering in all our ears.

"God, I wish I could shoot this," said Robin.

"Make a deal with Hubbard."

She wrinkled her nose.

Sonny came back, grinning. He'd lost some cool, he seemed a little dazed.

Robin asked, "What did Ali say?"

"'Trust in God and don't get hit.'"

"Sounds good to me," said Alfred.

"Great warrior," said Jake. "Stood for what he believed."

We settled down for the fight. John L. was sweating before the opening bell. His forehead was red. There were red streaks on his chest.

"Too hot for an old man," said Jake.

John L. stuck to his plan. He moved right out at the bell and tried to crowd Junior so he couldn't box and dance, he tried to bull him toward a corner, and he kept flicking out left jabs to keep him off balance. But Junior was a disciplined fighter, you could see right away that he also had a plan: Watch out for John L.'s right hand and keep moving back to the middle of the ring where there was plenty of room to dance the old man into exhaustion.

The first round was slow; they were feeling each other out, a few rights and hooks that didn't quite land. I scored it even. When it was over John L. plopped down on his stool as if he was tired already.

"He's melting," Robin said.

Junior picked up the pace in the second round, throwing a jab, moving his head, skipping out of range of John L.'s counterpunch.

105

Twice, John L. threw roundhouse rights that got the crowd roaring, but Junior caught them both high on his arms. They must have hurt— you could hear the damp smack—but they didn't land anywhere they would do damage. Toward the end of the round, John L. bulled in and tried to throw some inside punches, but Junior locked his elbows to his sides and pushed him off.

I hated to admit it, but Junior was a strong fighter with all the right moves. He wasn't exciting to watch, but he made no mistakes. He was so well trained that he had an answer for everything. He knew how to avoid the right hand, slide off the ropes, clutch and run.

"He's a robot," I said. "RoboPug. No fire, no passion."

"But he's good," said Sonny.

"And he's going to win," said Robin.

She was right. First John L.'s legs slowed down, then his arms sagged. Junior became less cautious, skipping forward and landing combinations. It was like hitting soft clay. John L.'s flesh didn't spring right back. His face started to lump up. His chest and arms were splotchy.

John L. didn't sit down between rounds.

"Trying to psyche Junior," I said. "Show he doesn't need to sit down."

"Can't sit down," said Robin. "Knows he won't get up again."

Alfred said, "He's gone."

John L. was too tired to get out of the way; he could only absorb the punishment and try to punch back. But he had to take three punches to land one, and after a while he was staggering after Junior like a drunk.

"He's out on his feet," said Alfred.

"Oughta stop it," said Sonny.

People in our section were moaning and looking away, but the rest of the arena was chanting for the kill, "JUN-ior, JUN-ior." John L.'s skin was bright red, his mouth and nose were torn and bloody, his eyes were swelling shut, but he wouldn't quit, wouldn't go down.

"Why doesn't the ref stop it?" said Sonny. His face was covered with beads of perspiration; his fists were pale.

Between rounds, Richie was screaming and John L. was shaking his head. He wouldn't let Richie stop it.

I heard heavy breathing next to me. Sonny

was sucking air through his mouth, wincing at every blow.

In the seventh round, Junior backed John L. into a corner and began chopping at his head, a lumberjack killing a tree with his axe, and the crowd screamed for Junior to pour it on. Only the ropes were keeping John L. up.

"Stop it," shouted Sonny.

He hurtled down the aisle, snatching the white towel off Richie's shoulder on the run, throwing it ahead of him into the ring. Security guards tried to pull him back, but all they could do was tear the shirt off his back. Sonny leaped over the ropes and brushed the referee aside and threw himself between the fighters. He wrapped his arms around John L. and pushed him into his corner.

The arena exploded, people yelling, surging forward. Robin and I started for the ring, got caught in the swirl and were knocked back, but when Sonny came tumbling out of the ring with five security guys on top of him, we jumped on the pile and tried to pull them off.

Suddenly a familiar voice roared, "LET THE BOY UP!"

It was Elston Hubbard, Senior, himself,

peeling the guards off Sonny and throwing them away like banana skins. He pulled Sonny to his feet.

"You crazy, boy."

Sonny swung at him, but Senior ducked and wrapped up Sonny's arms. Sonny relaxed, and Senior hugged him. "You did the right thing," he said, and shoved Sonny into my arms. "Writer-Boy, take him before he gets hurt."

Sonny let me drag him away. Robin and Jake and I linked arms around Sonny, and Alfred cleared a path for us back to the dressing room. We were there when John L. was carried in and laid out on the rubbing table.

"Heat exhaustion," said the ring doctor. "Happened to Sugar Ray Robinson, happens to the best of them."

John L. struggled up. "Who stopped the goddamn fight? I woulda won, woulda knocked . . ." He collapsed.

Richie began to cry.

17

ONNY AND I RODE the ambulance to the hospital. John L. was babbling in Yiddish, delirious. Richie cradled his head in his lap. The emergency-room doctor took one look at John L. and stuck an intravenous needle into his arm. That's when I bailed out. I sat in the waiting room until John L. was admitted to the hospital for observation. Richie said he would sleep in his room overnight. He made us leave.

When we got back to the hotel, Jake and Alfred and Robin were waiting for us in a suite. There was food and champagne on the table.

"Nothing to celebrate," grumbled Sonny.

"Hubbard sent them," said Alfred. "You're the big winner tonight."

"Every TV station in the country ran you stopping the fight," said Robin.

"Gotta go," said Sonny. He turned away.

"Where?" asked Alfred.

"Gotta run." He was out the door.

We talked for a while, about Sonny's killer hook, John L.'s condition. We ate some food and zapped the TV for glimpses of Sonny stopping the fight. It would be on everybody's year-end reel. After a while Alfred went off to bed; you could see on his face he was fighting pain. Robin made plans with Jake to go up to the Res with her crew. Then Jake drifted away. I sat there with Robin and not much to talk about.

"So. You're going to shoot the roots thing."

"I'll want to interview you, too, how you met Sonny, the Rocky bit. But I'll do that at Donatelli's."

"What makes you so sure I want to be interviewed?"

She smiled, all teeth, no warmth. "Good pub for your book."

"I don't need some documentary in the middle of the night on educational television to sell a book on the heavyweight champion of the world."

"Right. All you need is the champion. And I can see you're sticking pretty close."

"He's my friend." I stood up.

"And you saw him first." She stood up. "Look, Marty, there's plenty of room for both of us. We're doing different things."

"I need to get back so I can write all that down." I wanted to leave before she gave me the eyebrows.

"We can help each other. I think I understand how you feel." Her voice was softer, warmer. The eyebrows never moved. "You paid your dues for two years on the road, all those crappy little towns, and now I waltz in when things look hot. Right?"

"Wrong," I lied.

Now the eyebrows rose. She really pushed my buttons, but I wasn't sure if it was the alarms or the warms. I was trying to think of an exit line when Hubbard made his entrance. Just burst into the suite, talking.

"I like this, the writer and the filmmaker, plotting out how to carve the facts into legend." He was wearing a T-shirt that bore the words. THE BIG BANG: JUNIOR HUBBARD COLLIDES WITH SONNY BEAR. "Press conference at ten A.M. in the ballroom downstairs. Announce the next fight. Make sure Sonny's there." He poked himself in the chest. "Ordered this shirt as The Fave went down."

"You talk to Alfred about this?"

"Details. Got to have the big vision. You can always work out the details."

"Like getting a tape of Sonny stopping the Solomon fight for my documentary?" asked Robin.

"Just a detail," said Hubbard. "You know, I never been happy with my video people. We got to talk."

"I'm ready."

I don't think they noticed me leaving the room.

Sonny didn't come back until after sunup. He looked as though he had run for hours. His eyes were buried in his head, his clothes were black with sweat. The only other time I remembered him looking so wild was the night Alfred got shot and we went hunting the guy who did it. "You okay?"

"They're selling T-shirts downstairs. THE BIG BANG." He collapsed on the bed. "I'd like to take that sonuvabitch right now."

18

I WROTE HARD. TRIED to stick to a schedule. Up early, write for three hours, down to Donatelli's for lunch with Henry or one of the other trainers to check out facts, then back for another three or four hours at the computer. I'd fall asleep watching TV.

After a few days I began taking longer and longer TV breaks, then naps in the afternoon, and then I'd stay up all night pounding the keyboard and be too tired to go to the gym. I started bringing in pizza and fried chicken. I had the apartment to myself—Denise was a counselor at a camp for retarded kids for the summer and my folks were traveling—so it was easy to live around the clock.

It was in the back of my mind to have some people over—a girl I liked from school was in town—but I was in a writing mode, hammering out pages, eating, sleeping, watching some TV to chill, then back to the hammer. My pants were getting tighter from too much takeout.

I wasn't sure if my pages were good. Some days I liked them and some days they read like Dead White Male meets Oreo Kid. I'd get panicky then and listen to rap on TV or go talk with the school-yard ball players and dope dealers I knew from elementary school. I never had much trouble with them; my father was a neighborhood hero who made it and stayed in the community, and since Las Vegas, I'd started to get a little respect on my own. Everybody figured I had my own gangsta connections.

I never worked so hard in my life. Writing was always fun for me, especially when I was making up stories, but this had to be just right: The facts and the observations had to be true because these were real people I was writing about, and the sentences had to sing and dance because I wanted those real people to think I was a contender, too. Sometimes I felt like I was training for my own Big Bang.

It took two weeks, nonstop, to get the chapters in shape for Professor Marks. I left the early chapters in the present tense because I liked the way it gets you right into the story. Besides, I wasn't going to roll over for him.

I thought I might have made the cut over Sonny's left eye more of a mythical wound, like an Achilles' heel, the symbol for his tragic flaw. Professors usually are suckers for pseudointellectual Greek stuff. Maybe not Marks. Weren't the Greeks your classic dead white males? Besides, what was Sonny's tragic flaw, other than he didn't know who he was yet?

Who did?

Not me.

But by chapter 5 I thought I was emerging as a character in my own book. Marks was right about that being necessary. I began to feel better about the pages as I read on. The reservation stuff was okay, particularly the scenes with Sonny in chapter 9.

Vegas took off for me. The little comments to Marks seemed like childish graffiti, but they had helped me keep an attitude while I wrote. It was like the scaffolding outside a building under construction, something to stand on while you were working. You tore it down when the building was finished. I could always delete those remarks in the final draft. Marks would surely want a polish, those guys always do. It's a power thing.

I wondered if I should have reported more on the trouble brewing on the Res. Always time to deal with that if it boils over. I thought I showed that boxing stank without getting preachy about it. It was all there, except maybe I hadn't really spelled out my feelings about Sonny. Did it read as if I was just hanging on for the big payday, my best-seller?

I mailed the chapters to Rumson Lake, New York, where Marks was spending the summer. Talk about coincidence—forty years ago my dad spent a couple of weeks with a white family up there as a Fresh Air kid.

I thought I'd feel great, relieved and light, after I sent out the chapters, but I felt empty and tired. Hung over.

I took a bus up to the Res, looking forward to a few days of relaxing in the sunny quiet. I'd never seen the place so crowded and noisy. First of all, there wasn't even room for me to sleep at Jake's. Robin and her crew had filled the little yellow house with TV gear. I had to bunk with three little kids in the house of Alice Benton, the Stump Clan Mother.

The afternoon I got to the Res, Robin was directing a scene in which Sonny and Jake walked through the junkyard, searching for an auto part someone from Sparta had ordered. They worked together a lot when Sonny was a kid. Because the sun kept reflecting off the windshields of the old wrecks and into the camera, Robin and her crew shot the scene over and over.

Finally, I said, "What's this, a documentary or a major motion picture?"

"Relax," said Sonny. "We haven't sold the book rights, still yours."

Everybody laughed. But just him saying that stressed me out. Sonny never thought of things like that. Was Robin looking to snag the book, too?

I felt shut out. That night, when I went back to the Clan Mother's house, Robin and Sonny were still planning the next day's shoot. I wondered if she and Sonny were getting it on.

In the morning, Jake came out in his old leather breechcloth and demonstrated the stick dance, kicking twigs from instep to instep for the camera. He'd taught that to Sonny to improve his footwork and coordination.

And then, while Robin smiled and nodded him on, he babbled away about the old days on the Res when he hunted for food, about the Running Braves, about corrupt chiefs who had sold out the Nation, all the stories I'd worked so hard to coax out of him when I used to come up here with my notebooks and tape recorder, following Jake for hours, begging him to sit down and be interviewed.

During a break, I said to Robin, "Amazing how everybody loves to be on TV."

She arched the famous eyebrows. "Different media, Marty. You can be a fly on the wall, but I have to have pictures. Believe me, we are not in competition." She looked at her watch. "We're going up to Stonebird this afternoon, you should come along."

That's when I decided to go home. The three-day solo of survival and meditation had become a three-hour mob-scene shoot.

When I stopped to get my bag, Alice Benton was standing over the stove in a fragrant cloud of steam. The house was quiet; her three grandkids were still in school.

"Thanks for your hospitality," I said. "I'm leaving now."

"I'll drive you to town. After you eat."

By the time I washed up and sat down,

there was a big bowl of soup on the table, and a hunk of bread.

"It's great." The soup had different tastes on different parts of my tongue.

"Traditional recipe. Long-distance runners carried it in leather flasks."

"The Running Braves?"

"Jake tell you about them?"

"Says we need them." I wondered why I said "we."

"Need something. Gonna be trouble."

"You really think so?"

"I've never seen the Moscondaga people so split. The people who leased their land to the gambling company think it's their right. And that it's their only chance for a good life. The people who think all the land belongs to all the people think that gambling will destroy the Nation."

"You think gambling's a bad thing?"

"Good or bad, might be too late to stop it. Question is How we going to control it so it doesn't destroy the Nation? People are ready to shoot each other over this."

On the ride out of the Res, I heard bulldozers and backhoes snarling, saw trucks and construction trailers and a glittery circle of barbed wire. Guards with guns and dogs and walkie-talkies patrolled inside the fence while workers mounted closed-circuit TV cameras on a watch-tower.

"Wait'll Jake sees this," I said.

"He better be careful," said Alice Benton.

I bought a pile of magazines at the bus station, so I wouldn't have to think about Robin and Sonny and the Moscondaga for a few hours. But whenever I finished a magazine article, I'd think about being alone and feel sad. I kept reminding myself that at least things couldn't get much worse.

Wrong again. At home, there was a message on the answering machine from Professor Marks. "Register for classes." He'd turned down my chapters. No independent study. It was over for me.

It's time to hang it up. Who wants to be a writer anyway? This is how Sonny must have felt after the Viera fight. I thought I should make notes on how I was feeling, so I could understand him better, but then I remembered that I wasn't a writer anymore.

19

I WAS BACK AT SCHOOL feeling sorry for myself when some guy I hardly knew sat down next to me in the Morris Dining Hall and asked, "What's your favorite kosher vegetable?"

"Huh?"

"John L. Solomon." When nobody at the table laughed, he said, "Didn't hear the news?"

"Martin knows him," said one of the other guys.

"Sorry, I didn't mean . . ."

"What happened?" I'd been in the library all day.

"He's in a coma. Something burst in his brain."

Big story that night. The news programs had their doctor reporters explaining what happened inside John L.'s head and their commentators arguing whether or not boxing should be abolished. John L. had seemed all right after the Hubbard fight; he'd made some appearances and started talking about another fight. He even began training again. While he was jogging along the boardwalk near his house, he collapsed. One reporter stood on the spot where he fell. Someone had stuck flowers between the gray wooden boards.

I wanted to talk to someone that night, but Jake and Sonny were already driving down from the Res. Alice said they'd heard the news. Alfred was in the hospital; the chronic bowel infection some paraplegics get had flared. My folks were at meetings, and Robin's machine said she'd call right back but she didn't.

I didn't want to talk to other kids at school. I felt superior to them in some ways—they'd never carried a spit bucket and wiped blood—but inferior, too. I was back at school because I was a loser.

Before I thought it through, I called Professor Marks. I hadn't seen him since I got back to school.

"Yes?" He sounded as if I had interrupted him.

"Sorry to bother you. This is Martin Witherspoon . . ."

"I have office hours tomorrow. Two to three."

"Uh, okay . . . I, er, you hear about John L. Solomon?"

"No."

"Well, it's on the news—he's in a coma, he . . ."

"Come on over right now," said Professor Marks. He gave me his address.

He lived in a dumpy apartment a few blocks from the dorms. He was wearing jeans and a T-shirt and he was barefoot. I followed him into a small living room. Books and papers were scattered over soft chairs.

"Coffee, soda?"

"Nothing, thanks, sure, anything." I suddenly wondered why I was here.

"There's no alcohol. I'm, uh, writing dry this year." He cracked open two bottles of some kind of natural fruit drink I'd never seen before. It didn't taste very good.

"Your John L. chapters were interesting. His confusion about his Jewishness."

"He didn't seem confused to me."

"Sure he was. He wore his Jewishness instead of living it. Good parallel to Sonny's emerging sense of himself as a Moscondaga."

"But you rejected it."

124

"I rejected your leaving school to try to write a best-seller before you were ready."

"What do you mean?"

"You've got talent. I've read your stories in the literary magazine. The stuff you did in the screenplay class."

"Then why did you . . ."

"You've got to finish school. You need the training, the little fights. Keep writing your book. A real writer writes, in school, in jail, underwater, whatever. Most people quit. That's the truth. The people who win aren't necessarily the ones with the most talent. They're the ones who never stopped coming."

I felt confused. "What should I do?"

"You want to be where the action is." He looked at his watch. "Probably make the last train to New York. Take notes. Don't miss too many classes. Get back as soon as you can."

20

SONNY WAS THERE when John L. died. He was
in the hospital room with Richie and John
L.'s second ex-wife and their daughters
when John L. opened his eyes, smiled, and
closed them again. There were stories in the
paper that John L. died with his fist inside
Sonny's fist, and that his last words were "Take
Hubbard for me," but Sonny said that was just
Hubbard Senior hyping the next fight.

Jews get buried right away. Sonny and
Richie were honorary pallbearers along with
some bearded men in black cloth coats. TV
cameras pushed in on the coffin. Sonny was
cool. He said that John L. was a great champion
and a great friend, but that he didn't blame anybody for his death, certainly not Elston
Hubbard, Junior. It was a risk that fighters
took.

Senior was all over that funeral. He said he
understood that Sonny needed to avenge John

126

L.'s death and fight Junior. "It's nothing personal. When a man's chief falls, there must be satisfaction. That is the way of the warrior."

The press ate that up, and started writing about a "grudge match," and how the fight might not even get licensed if the commission thought Sonny was out for revenge. Sonny stayed at my folks' apartment for a few days, and the phone never stopped ringing with calls from the press. After a while, Sonny started getting impatient with the reporters asking the same questions over and over. He said he might want revenge on Senior for talking trash. When that was quoted, Junior said he was going to knock out Sonny for bad-mouthing his dad. After that, I handled the press calls. No comment. Thanks. No comment.

Sonny ran in the mornings in the park along the Hudson River, and I followed him on my bike. Neighborhood kids started trailing us. Sonny got a kick out of that, which surprised me. He'd fool around with them, show them some footwork, how to throw the hook. He was even getting more relaxed with adults. He liked being recognized on the street. Women were hitting on him all the time. A few nights he didn't come home, but we never asked him about it. Denise said she thought he might have stayed at Robin's house, but she might have said that to needle me.

Every day we worked on Rocky. Sonny made that sucker dance, snapping out the jab, straight as a line drive, twisting his fist on impact.

"Jab . . . five. Hook . . . seven."

We mixed punches, built combinations, using the jab to keep the opponent off balance, the hook and the right for power blows.

"Jab . . . five. Hook . . . seven."

Start a pattern, let the opponent get into a rhythm of what to expect.

"Jab . . . five."

Then, "Right . . . eight. Hook . . . nine."

"Good work," I said. "I like the way you moved your head after the punch."

He grinned at me. He knew what I was doing. He hadn't been moving his head properly at all, but you can't yell at a hardhead like Sonny—you have to use psychology. I learned that from Alfred. And a smart hardhead like Sonny likes it when you jerk his string. Means you know what you're doing.

Whenever Sonny climbed into the ring, other fighters and trainers stopped working out to watch. I greased Sonny's face and slipped on the headgear. Dave the Fave climbed in. He was one of Sonny's biggest boosters now. He'd gotten good security-guard jobs from the publicity of their Vegas fight, and he loved to boast about being the guy who gave Sonny his start. Henry let him train for free in exchange for sparring with Sonny, which could be fun if you didn't mind being punched around. Sonny wasn't one of those hothouse fighters who have to be treated carefully in the gym. You could whale at him if you were willing to take a whack back.

Sonny was doing most of the whaling the day Hubbard Senior showed up. He climbed up on the ring apron and leaned on the ropes next to me.

"Your boy needs better'n Dave to get sharp."

"Isn't this a conflict of interest?" I asked.

"How you mean?" His brow was all wrinkled as if he didn't know what I was talking about. Fat snake.

"It's your son fighting, and you're the promoter, and now you're here giving his opponent advice. I don't get it."

"Ah, boxing, it's like poetry," said Hubbard. "Mysterious. Once you try to explain it, poof, the magic is gone."

"I better write that down," I said sarcastically.

He nodded. "Sometimes I say things, I wish I had me a writer so I don't lose 'em. In fact"—he reached into a pocket and pulled out a roll of bills as big as his fist—"I could advance you . . ."

"I should have you thrown out like you had us thrown out. You're a spy."

"Chill, boy. Your friend Robin had a financial problem and I . . ."

"Robin?"

The bell rang, and Sonny sauntered over. "You here to set the date?"

"Could be. The public's panting to see the two best young heavyweights in the world."

"I've got a manager," said Sonny. "You better talk to him."

"Be glad to talk to anyone," said Senior. "But I want to be sure you are properly represented by someone who knows the nooks and the crannies of a world populated by people of devious disposition."

"You already announced the fight in Vegas," I said.

"Not the details," said Hubbard. "You get to fight Junior if you sign with me as promoter for your next three fights."

"That way, you get a sure rematch after Sonny wins," I said.

"Right on, brother." Hubbard threw back his head and gave off an annoying howl. He dug into his pocket and came out with the roll. He peeled off bills, crumpled them and stuffed them down the front of Sonny's trunks. "Get yourself a fly suit for the signing ceremony."

"I didn't say I'd sign."

"Armani be fine." He swaggered to the door.

Sonny didn't even look at the money until we got back to the apartment. At dinner, after I told the story, he asked my dad, "How much does an Armani suit cost?"

"That depends," said my dad, who doesn't like people to think he doesn't know everything.

"At least two *K*," said Denise.

Sonny grinned at me. "Get one for you, too. That was five grand he gave me."

Denise clapped her hands. "Party time."

I did my geek impression. "Wall to wall babes."

Mom said, "You can't walk around with that . . ."

Dad said, "That's bad money. Strings attached."

"Sonny made no promises," I said.

"Better talk to Alfred," said Dad.

He was in the hospital. He tried to hide the feeding tube in his stomach and the urinary catheter coming out between his legs. He couldn't hide the deep pain lines across his forehead. Sonny laid out the details of Hubbard's visit.

I said, "The deal stinks."

Alfred said, "But it's pretty cut and dried. You need Junior to move up. Senior's the only one can deliver."

"I don't trust Hubbard," said Sonny.

"Who does?" said Alfred. "But it's his way or the highway."

21

I F THE LAS VEGAS gambling hotels are an oasis in the desert, then the Atlantic City gambling hotels are an oasis in hell, surrounded by houses that look like tombstones, empty lots carpeted with broken glass, junkies, crack kids, muggers, beggars, whores. Robin and her crew spent one whole morning trying to get a single shot of Sonny running along the boardwalk, the sand and the ocean on his left, the hotels on his right, the slums behind him. The idea was that Sonny was running from a hopeless ghetto toward gambling casinos where you could change your life in one lucky night. I told her I thought the shot was crap because the casinos were a mirage. Ultimately nobody ever won.

She laughed. "You don't understand television."

"I understand reality."

"Television is emotion, quick impressions, a few seconds to leave an imprint on the brain.

133

You're thinking linear." She reached into her bag and pulled out a pack of cigarettes. "End of lecture. Can you afford to take so much time off school?"

"Since when did you start smoking?"

"I think this is all getting to me."

"What? The documentary? Atlantic City? Sonny? Hubbard's money?"

She lit the cigarette and turned her head to blow the smoke away from me. "You going to flunk out?"

"You going to sell out?"

"You don't know anything about reality, either, kid." She tossed the cigarette and stalked back to her crew.

We spent the week in A-City to drum up publicity for the pay-per-view boxing show. It was all about getting stories in newspapers and on TV. Sonny was getting better, but he was no Mr. Soundbite, and Junior Hubbard was dead from the neck up, so everybody in both camps pitched in giving interviews. That was the deal: keep the fighters sharp and the media fed.

So there were stories about Hubbard being a tool of the Mafia, about Richie being on a vendetta against Junior because of John L.'s death, about Jake channeling the souls of dead warrior chiefs to give Sonny supernatural strength. The only story that was true was about a struggling filmmaker who got a grant from the Hubbards' nonprofit foundation to finish her video on machismo in boxing. Robin wouldn't discuss it with me.

The week went fast, but each day was long. Up early to run, nap, eat breakfast, walk and rest, work out, press conference, rest, watch fight films and talk strategy, eat, a few special interviews, sleep. Constant idle chatter to keep Sonny amused and focused on the fight, but not so intense he'd burn out. Richie was good at jokes and small talk, and Dave the Fave kept everybody laughing with his crazy raps. Clowns are essential at a fight camp.

Richie and Henry spent a lot of time going over the fight plan with Sonny, how he had to expect a long, tough fight because Junior was in good condition, how he had to respect Junior's right hand, how he couldn't get discouraged in the early rounds if Junior's defense seemed impregnable. Junior was a well-trained fighter, and disciplined. But he didn't have a lot of imagination, and when the big moment came, Sonny had to be ready to be creative and pour it on.

"Patient, then pounce," said Richie.

Sonny just nodded. You couldn't be sure exactly how much of it he was buying.

There was a little story in the paper about a shooting on the Res. The chiefs must have hushed it up and taken care of the wounded guy themselves, because there were no police or hospital reports. The print reporters started asking about Moscondaga politics. The TV reporters preferred Dave the Fave. They got him to do an "original" rap a TV producer wrote for him about the fight.

I didn't get to spend much time alone with Sonny. I wondered how he was reacting to John L.'s death. He never mentioned it. Sometimes I wondered just how well I really knew him. Was he stuffing it down, not dealing with it? Or had he cruised past it, John L. gone and forgotten?

The morning of the fight, Alfred drove down in his specially equipped HandiVan. He'd lost a lot of weight, and there were hollows in his cheeks. While Sonny napped, Alfred suggested we stroll the boardwalk. I was surprised. We've never been close; in fact I thought he didn't like me much, just tolerated me because my dad was a hero of his.

"How's school?"

"Okay."

"What?"

"I said, it's okay." It's not so easy walking and talking to someone in a wheelchair.

"Aren't you missing classes?"

I walked a little ahead of him and leaned down. "They're cutting me slack."

"You have to keep your own thing going, Marty. School, writing."

"My dad ask you to speak to me?"

"No, but I'm sure we feel the same way. I'm also thinking about Sonny. He's going to need you up the road. He's going to need a real friend."

"If he wins, he'll have plenty of friends," I said.

"He'll need old ones. Hang in there with him, Marty. Be some rough times."

"You think he's going to win?"

"Whatever happens, he's going to lose his

way for a while. He's not going to listen to any-body."

"Won't listen to me either."

"Count on it. But you can keep the door open so we can all come back when he's ready again."

"What does Jake think?"

"Same as I do," said Alfred. "'Cept he's got all those hawks and spirits on the case."

22

ONNY AND JUNIOR settled right into a steady, grinding fight, trying to wear each other down until the chance came to fire the big one. Patient, then pounce. They were both playing that game. They respected each other's knockout punch. The crowd booed because they were cautious.

I was sitting with my dad in great seats behind the press rows. He was grunting and moving along with Sonny. It was like virtual reality: Every time my father's left shoulder twitched, Sonny jabbed.

"What do you think?" I asked.

"Too early to tell," he said. "Both have the skill. We'll have to see who has the will. Will beats skill."

It wasn't the kind of fight the mob guys and the rap gangstas love, bing-bang-blood and good-night, but for anyone who really enjoyed and understood boxing it was state of the art, two disciplined fighters trying to dominate each other through strength and tactics.

I was proud of Sonny. He never got angry or lost control for a second, moving in with crisp jabs, dancing away from Junior's right hand, moving his head after he threw a punch, spinning off the ropes, wasting no energy with macho moves or insults. He kept up the pressure on Junior without leaving himself open for a big punch. My dad was impressed, too.

"He's learned a lot. He's been paying attention."

"He's going to win," I said.

"Senior's worried."

Between rounds, Senior pressed his mouth to Junior's ear and talked until the bell rang, then slapped him hard on the back to get him going.

But Junior knew only one way to fight. Dig it out. He was a laborer with a pick and shovel—give him enough time, he'll dig the hole and bury you. It had worked with everyone else he had ever fought, because he was stronger or in better condition or more disciplined—everyone else cracked under Junior's relentless forward march and did something stupid that left him open for the dynamite right.

Except Sonny. Cool and deadly Sonny, stick and move, willing to fight this dull, grinding, brutal fight.

In his corner, Richie and Alfred kept up a steady stream of coaching and cheerleading, and Jake sponged his face and washed his mouthpiece. Every so often, Robin and her crew moved in for close-ups.

In the middle of the sixth round, Dad whispered, "He's got 'im." Sonny was in command, moving Junior backward with sharp jabs that couldn't be brushed aside, pounding him into the ropes. Sonny had the will. Junior began dancing and grinning to hide his panic, but he couldn't keep his arms up and he was grunting at body blows.

Between rounds, Alfred and Richie were screaming at Sonny to go for it, and Senior was yelling at Junior and tapping his left eyebrow.

I had a flashback . . . Iron Pete Viera.

Junior threw a right at Sonny's left eye, and when Sonny batted it away, Junior crossed with a left, missed and clinched. He rammed his head into Sonny's face. As the referee broke them, Junior took another swipe at the eye. The referee warned him, but the damage was done.

141

The old scar tissue was leaking blood. How had he known about the cut?

"Here's where the fix comes in," I said. "Doctor calls it, Junior wins, Senior still has rights to the rematch."

"Let's try not to be paranoid." Dad must have been thinking the same thing.

After the seventh, Jake and Richie managed to seal the leak by pinching the flesh hard, then fingering ointment into it. Alfred, hanging on the ropes, was shouting new instructions. Sonny would have to protect that eye now, without losing his momentum. It would be tough.

For most of the eighth round, I thought he could do it. He was still sharp, bulling Junior around the ring, snapping out the jab, maneuvering him into position for the left hook.

"Just two more rounds and we're home free," I babbled. "He must be ahead on points."

"Can't be sure," said Dad. "He can't lay back now."

A good right cross turned Junior's face into a fair left hook and he fell back against the ropes, clutching at Sonny, who stumbled forward into a clinch, another butt, and suddenly blood was running down into his eye. Sonny stepped back and his blood sprayed out onto the reporters' notebooks and laptops. The crowd roared at the blood.

If the bell had rung then, and if Jake had had a chance to close the cut again . . .

The doctor rushed into the ring, signaling the referee, and the two of them examined Sonny's eye, and then Senior and Junior were hugging. It was over. A technical knockout for Hubbard. A robbery. Iron Pete Viera.

But this time Sonny didn't vault the ropes and stalk out of the arena. He swept the doctor and the referee aside and charged across the ring.

In slow motion, the Hubbards separated to meet him, their hands up.

Sonny decked Junior with a beautiful left hook, sharp, short, on the button. Hook . . . 1.

The hook that put Senior away was longer, not so hard, but good enough. Hook . . . 7.

The scene is frozen in my mind. The Hubbards stretched out at his feet, Sonny turns to face the world, his fists cocked. But there is no one left to hit.

The picture made him famous. He flew out to Hollywood with Jake the next day.

23

JAKE LEFT HOLLYWOOD after a few days, but I was too busy at school to visit him until Thanksgiving break. He didn't pick me up at the Sparta bus station, so I took a taxi to his house. The Res throbbed with the grind and snarl of heavy machinery, bulldozers, backhoes, hammering, chain saws, workers' boomboxes. When I passed the construction site, a guard followed the cab with the point of his rifle.

Jake was in the junkyard digging a hole to bury Custer. He was wearing his big old Colt on his hip.

"What happened?"

"Poisoned."

"Who did it?"

He jerked a thumb toward the rising cloud of construction dust.

"Moscondaga wouldn't do that," I said.

Jake stopped, leaned on his shovel and spat.

"Moscondaga just as bad as anyone else when they forget where they come from. Think a gambling casino's gonna make 'em white." He handed me the shovel.

I finished digging the hole. It was hard work. I was wet and whipped when we finally lowered Custer in and covered him with dirt. Jake mumbled words I didn't understand and sprinkled dried herbs over the grave.

"What are you going to do?"

"Nothin'. Up to the chiefs."

"You're not going to do anything?"

"Not gonna start a war, get Moscondaga killing each other."

"Where do you stand?"

He waved his skinny arms around the junk-yard. "Right here with the old wrecks."

"I'm serious."

He wheezed and sat down on a rotting old backseat. "Not so simple. Moscondaga gamble. Running Braves used to race each other, people bet on that. What's tearing the Nation apart is people from the outside waving big money, turning us against each other.

"White people did the same thing a hundred years ago, two hundred years ago, get us drunk and make the chiefs sign treaties. Moscondaga needs outside money for roads, schools, clinic. But if the Nation's not together, outside money means outside control, and then we lose what we got."

"What's the answer?"

"Two sides got to come together, talk it out. Too late to stop gambling. Got to find a way to keep control of it. Someone got to bring us together."

I knew the answer but I asked the question anyway. "Who can do it?"

"Running Brave could do it." He made the sign of the Running Brave, a fist with the thumb coming up between third and the ring fingers. "From the People, when the People need him."

"You think Sonny can do it?"

He snorted. "Not Sonny Hollywood."

Jake hated Hollywood. Over dinner and into the night, he rambled on about his three days out there with Sonny.

"Think they love Indians," he said. "Want to pet us. Keep us in the doghouse till it's time to go on some show. Party."

"What did you do out there?"

"Eat mostly. Breakfast meetings, lunch meetings, dinner meetings. Party meetings. Everybody got some idea for a show around Sonny. Boxer, sheriff, one show he's the ghost of Black Hawk come back to save the Res."

"Who gets these ideas?"

"White guys, say they want to make up for all those westerns where we got killed. Long as they pay for all the meals, 's okay by me." He started laughing so hard he began to cough.

After a while, when he caught his breath, he said, "If they knew who Sonny was, they'd be afraid of him."

"Why?"

"He got the blood of the Running Braves. He's followed the Hawk. He could be a chief." He opened another beer.

"But why should they be afraid of him?"

"He's no pet, Sonny. Strong. Got his own mind, once he starts thinking."

Between Thanksgiving and Christmas the New England weather turned raw and mean, kicking up a wind that sliced through your clothes no matter what you were wearing. It was the time to burrow in, read and write, nail your courses, but I had trouble concentrating. I'd lucked into a single room in the dorms, but I turned into a hermit without using the time right. I watched TV for Sonny sightings, read the papers and magazines for Sonny mentions, and I ate too much. I was falling behind in my courses, especially my writing courses. I hated to turn anything in; I'd lost confidence. Marks was working with individual students, so it was easy to avoid him. He called me a couple of times, but I never called him back. I didn't call anybody. After a while no one called me, except for Denise and my folks. Friends stopped coming by.

Sonny wasn't bad on late-night talk shows. He smiled easily, and what little he said sounded smart. Hosts would run the clip of him knocking down the Hubbards and standing over them, looking around for someone else to hit, and Sonny would say, "Looks like Sonny's Last Stand," and the audience would go crazy.

When serious hosts tried to make it a metaphor for The Rising of the Red Man, Sonny would smile and say that sports wasn't the answer—Jim Thorpe was the greatest athlete America ever produced, and look what happened to him. He'd get applause for that. When the ESPN types asked him if he planned to fight again, he would remind them he was under suspension by various boxing commissions for hitting the Hubbards. He avoided answering the question.

He dressed TV Indian—beaded shirts, jeans, boots, a bandanna. I caught him once on a music video with Dung Beetle. He was wearing boxing shorts and moccasins and punching the heavy bag to the beat of a drum. For a Hollywood guy he looked in great shape, but I could see a softening along his beltline. He wasn't working out. According to the gossip columns he was getting all his exercise on the dance floor and in bed. He was running with a wild crowd. He was a passenger in a Jeep when a famous leading man was picked up for drunk driving.

All by myself, I started thinking too much. Is this where it ends up for Sonny? Chiefing in Hollywood, a new breed freeway Indian? Is this why I went ballistic in Vegas, the best thing I ever did? So he can sell out? Is he selling out? What's he getting? Isn't it his life? At least no one's hitting him.

I was mad at him and proud of him. And I missed him. I wondered if he ever thought of me.

My folks had a big Christmas dinner. Alfred and his wife and their two little girls showed up; so did Henry, his wife and sons. Jake came down. Robin stopped by with champagne; she was in New York for Christmas with her folks. But there was a big hollow place in the middle of the party.

Robin showed a videotape she had put together, a rough cut of her documentary. It started with the famous shot of Sonny standing over the Hubbards, and then went to flashbacks and interviews. Everybody laughed and applauded when Jake and Alfred and I came on screen.

When Iron Pete Viera opened the cut over Sonny's left eye, I saw my dad and Alfred exchange glances.

That was how Hubbard knew about the old cut. He had screened Robin's tapes. Was he looking for something to give Junior an edge, or did he just happen to see it? Whatever he paid her, it was worth it.

Robin left, and the party was winding down when Sonny called. Denise answered the phone. One by one, Jake and Alfred and Mom and Dad and Henry talked to him.

Finally, it was my turn. He sounded tired or mellow, wasted or lonely. I couldn't tell for sure anymore.

"How's it going?" he asked.

"Hangin'."

"No school, huh?"

"Not for another three weeks."

He laughed. "Man, this place is weird. Need a writer to describe it. So come on out, huh?"

I thought he was jiving. "Yeah, why not? Get me a three-picture deal. Young Black writers are hot these days."

"Redskins, too. Okay, see you soon."

"Hey, wait, what's going on?"

"Be a package for you tomorrow. Christmas present." Then his voice changed a little. "Come out, Marty." He sounded like he needed a friend.

24

I FLEW FIRST-CLASS to L.A. It's a good thing I don't like the taste of champagne, because the flight attendants were pouring it like water, and I would have been smashed by the time I got there. I watched the movie, dozed, sampled the music channels, enjoyed the great window seat, especially when we flew over the Rockies, and wondered if the other people in first class were rich or got a ticket from a friend.

There was a chauffeur—black uniform and cap—waiting at the arrival gate with a sign: MR. WITHERSPOON. He took my bags to a white stretch limo. There was a TV with a VCR in the back, the tape cued to the part in the Dung Beetle video where Sonny was pounding the heavy bag to the drum.

There was more champagne in a bucket at the hotel. A man in a tuxedo who was in charge of the bellman who carried my bags told me that Mr. Bear wanted me to be comfortable and to order anything I wanted from room service. He suggested the filet mignon, rare, with a California merlot wine. He said that Mr. Bear would be back soon. I ordered dinner and settled down to wait. The hotel TV had ten different pay-per-view movies. I ate and watched three before I fell asleep thinking that I could get used to this.

Sonny showed up the next afternoon. He looked different. Thinner but softer, smiley, a little spacey. I wondered if he was on anything, but I didn't ask. Not right away. "How you doing?"

"Great. What's going on?"

"Everybody missed you at Christmas."

"Yeah. Parties out here you wouldn't believe. Santa Claus carved out of . . ."

"Things are really screwed on the Res."

"What else is new?"

"I think Jake's in big trouble."

He nodded and lowered himself carefully into the couch, as if he was achy. "Jake's tough, he can handle it."

"They poisoned Custer."

He grunted and rocked. "When?"

"Around Thanksgiving."

His eyes narrowed. The rusty gears inside his head were grinding. "Like a month ago. Jake never said."

"You ever call him?"

"Who did it?"

"Don't know."

"What's Jake say?"

"He doesn't want to start a civil war."

Sonny nodded. He was waking up. "They want to shut him up. That was a warning. What did he say he's gonna do?"

"He's going to wait for the Running Braves to save the People."

He held up his hand. "I didn't bring you out here to bring me down."

"You asked me a question."

"Maybe that wasn't the right answer."

"Maybe you're brain dead."

"Maybe you're starting to listen to foot-prints like Jake."

"What if he needs you?"

"For what?"

I made the Running Brave fist.

"That's not me."

"What's you?"

"We'll see."

"Here?"

"Why not?"

I tried to get him to open up. "What about John L.?"

"What about him?" Sonny talked tough. "He's still dead."

A different limo, a black stretch, picked us up at the hotel and took us out to the studio. A guard at the gate peeked in, checked us off on his clipboard list, and saluted us through.

We drove through the back lot, which was just like in the movies, phony streets with false-front buildings and actors wandering around in costume and makeup. I saw a dying alien jam a muffin into what looked like a laser wound.

We got out at a cottage and walked around to the back where some white guys were playing three-on-three basketball. They wore raggedy T-shirts, baggy shorts and the newest pump-up aerodynamic basketball shoes.

Sonny and I watched for a while. Most of them were in their early thirties and they were playing hard, but clean. Except that one of them, a little older and heavier, could foul, travel, anything he wanted and no one called it. He would have been dead in my school yard, really dead, like nine-millimeter poisoning. Unless, of course, he was the head drug dealer, in which case he would be playing by his own set of rules, just like here.

After a few minutes, they stopped and the head drug dealer said, "Want a run?"

Sonny held up his hands and said, "Too rough for me," which got a laugh, and when the head guy held up the ball toward me, I said, "I'm the only Black guy in America who can't jump," which got a smaller laugh than Sonny's, but I could tell everybody liked that. I felt like an instant Uncle Tom.

The big guy tossed the ball behind his head, feinted a jab at Sonny and shook my hand. "I'm Harley. You must be the famous Martin Malcolm Witherspoon."

We all followed Harley into the cottage, past women typing on word processors and into a large room with a giant TV screen, sofas and chairs, pinball machines, a Coke machine, a rocking horse with a real leather saddle, and big yellow plastic water-guns shaped like Uzis. It looked like the ultimate suburban rec room for teenagers. The younger guys introduced themselves to me. There were two Garys, a Franny, a Nick, and a Welles. They all grabbed sodas and threw themselves onto the soft chairs. Harley spread out on the couch.

"We want to do something real here," said Harley. "A pilot for a series about modern Indians. It's about identity, about a young Indian torn between his people and making it in the white world."

"We want to call it *The Chief*," said one of the Garys.

Sonny looked at me. I was on the spot. I suddenly realized he'd brought me out to talk for him.

"That's pretty serious," I said. "Being a chief is a big responsibility."

"On the money," said the other Gary. "This would be a very responsible guy."

"Chiefs are usually pretty old—thirties, forties at least." As soon as I said it, I felt like I had stepped in it. They all looked at each other and chuckled. "I mean in terms of . . ."

"Speak with straight tongue, that's what you're here for," said Harley, and he milked his laughs by rolling his eyes.

"His youth is important," said the first Gary. He was the serious guy. "He represents the new Indian, sensitive to what's going on in the world, yet respectful of the tribe's position."

"Nation," I said. "Tribe is kind of a white word."

"That's useful," said Harley. They all nodded at me.

"You're thinking of Sonny for the title role?" I asked.

"We are committed to a Native American as the lead," said the first Gary. "We'd like it to be Sonny. He tells us you're his writer."

Welles said, "We could put you on one of our sitcom development teams. We have a lot of work out here."

I was figuring it out. Sonny must have asked them to pay my way out here, and they must have thought I would be helpful keeping Sonny in line. They were trying to use me. Just like Senior Hubbard.

"Lunch," said Harley.

We went to the studio commissary and sat down at a huge round table in the corner. I tried to stay cool and keep up with the conversation, but there were just too many pretty people wandering about, some of whom I had seen on TV.

"Think of *The Chief* as a bridge," said the first Gary. "He's as hip to the ways of the white government as to tribal, uh, the Nation's leadership. He's kind of a policeman on the Res."

"So he could carry a gun?" I asked.

Harley winked. "You are smart."

"A chief would never carry a gun," I said.

From the way they looked at each other, I could tell they didn't think I was so smart anymore. I said, "Maybe he could be the chief's son, and there's, like, conflict between the old ways and the new. There's controversy over garbage disposal, or gambling—big political issues on the Res these days. He wants to work with the white man, but the old chief doesn't trust anybody who isn't an Indian."

"Interesting," said Harley, but I could tell he was losing interest.

"It's critical," said the first Gary, "that the lead character be an authority figure, tough and competent, although also accessible, vulnerable, with a sense of humor."

I said, "He'd be a fun chief."

"Sarcasm is out," said Franny.

While the waitress took our orders and

flirted with Harley, I tried to make eye contact with Sonny. But his eyes were glazed. Nobody was home. When I ordered the grilled chicken salad, he said he'd have the same thing. He didn't like grilled chicken salad.

They forgot about us for a while and talked among themselves about some other pilot, a dramatic hour about a rock group that solves crimes between gigs. They were considering Dung Beetle. It was just like boxing: You try to tie up all the rising talent, and you don't really care who makes it so long as you have a piece of the winner.

We were almost done eating when I filled a silent moment. "What about the heavyweight title?" I said. "Sonny's still a boxer."

"He's more than a boxer," said Harley. "He's a role model. He has the chance to do something really positive here. Educate America."

Sonny cleared his throat. "We've been educating you for five hundred years and you keep flunking the course."

They all laughed, a little too hard. It was like Sonny's Shakespeare crack. When you least expected it, he came up with a big one. I gave him the Running Braves fist. He shook his head.

We went back to the cottage, and there was more talk and a promise to get together again when there was a script, and then some other guys came for a meeting and we climbed back into the limo.

"What did you think?" I asked.

Sonny shrugged. "More bull artists. Let's see what they come up with."

We went back to the hotel, and Sonny went to sleep. I walked around the suite, watched TV, went downstairs, bought papers and magazines, hung around the pool, thought about trying to pick up a great-looking girl I saw and felt relieved when some studly guy sat down on her chaise. She wouldn't have been interested anyway. I went back upstairs and fell asleep.

Sonny woke me up around ten, and we went to a party. I thought drugs were over in Hollywood, but people kept disappearing and coming back. I didn't do any drugs; I felt responsible to keep a clear head for Sonny. I don't think Sonny did any either, at least not while I was watching. But who knows? I ate a lot of food and looked down the dresses of a lot of women who let me do it because I was a friend of Sonny's, and I talked to a very tall guy who used to play for the Lakers. I couldn't remember his name and it seemed insulting to ask.

We slept until two P.M., and went down for breakfast by the hotel pool. We stretched out in the sun and read the papers. Sonny spotted an article about himself. "Everybody's got an idea who I should be."

"Who should you be?"

"Don't ask me. I'm the only one doesn't know."

He dove into the pool. When he got out, I said, "Come on back with me. Get into shape. A tune-up fight, then the champ."

"I'm under suspension."

"No big deal. Dad says they'll have a hearing and announce that they're fining you, but they'll never collect it because boxing's in trouble. They need a star. Nobody's interested in Junior or the Wall. You could be the youngest heavyweight champion of all time."

"You got it all figured out." He sounded angry. "That's why you came out."

"You invited me, remember?"

"Maybe I just don't want to get punched

around anymore for nothing, keep getting robbed, going nowhere."

"This is nowhere."

"So go home."

"Maybe I will. Watch you chiefing it on TV."

"This Indian stuff. My dad was a white man from Minnesota."

"So wear lumberjack clothes on those dumb talk shows."

He got up and walked away.

That night I stayed in the hotel while Sonny went to a party at Harley's beach house. I couldn't sleep, trying to decide to stay or go home. He needed me. But I was just a third second.

I had a couple of weeks before school started again, and the weather was a lot better here than in the northeast. It wasn't a bad life if I could keep my mouth shut. Probably couldn't for too long. Maybe I should try, for Sonny's sake.

Then I thought about what Alfred had said before the Atlantic City fight. Keep the door open. Did that mean I should stay?

But Alfred also said I had to keep my own thing going. School, writing. Now I understood

163

what he meant: I could only be a real friend to Sonny if I wasn't dependent on him, if it didn't matter what he did because I was strong in what I did.

I didn't need him to box for me to write. And we both had to come back off the floor. I suddenly wished I had brought my laptop. I wanted to get it all down.

Before dawn I went for a swim, which didn't help me make up my mind. When I got back to the room, there was an urgent message to call Robin.

They'd shot Jake.

25

I FOUND SONNY SPRAWLED on a pile of cushions next to Harley's pool. He looked dead. I thought about rolling him into the pool as a wake-up call, but if he went down, I might never get him up again. So I walked him around the pool, around and around, until the sun came up. He was leaning on me at first, then staggering and groaning.

"Gon' barf," he said.

"Go for it." I pointed him over the pool. It came out in one long silver rainbow and splashed into the water. "That's good, chief. Vulnerable but tough."

I could write better dialogue than those creeps, even if I couldn't play basketball with them.

Sonny's clothes were scattered. Getting him dressed took a while. There were some other people in the pool house, waking up slowly. I was cool and didn't stare at them, although I was almost sure I had seen one of the women on MTV.

The limo driver was waiting patiently for us out in the driveway, reading an Arabic newspaper. When I loaded Sonny into the back, he barely looked up. I had a feeling he'd seen all this before, and worse.

I thought we'd have trouble getting out of the hotel, but the studio had guaranteed payment, and at the airport I exchanged the return flight of my first-class ticket for two economy tickets. I left a message on Robin's machine with our flight number and time of arrival. Sonny slept most of the way home. Somewhere around Chicago he woke up and filled a barf bag. I got him some water and he felt better and then he went back to sleep.

Robin was waiting for us at JFK. We tucked Sonny into the back of her old BMW and covered him with a blanket.

"He looks awful," she said.

"He had the total Hollywood experience. Did everything, did everybody, and now he's done."

"That sounds like a line you'll put in your book and a good editor will take out."

"I'll put it back," I said. "How's Jake?"

"The wound isn't so serious, but they're worried about his heart. He's in the hospital in Sparta."

"Let's go."

Sonny slept in the back most of the way up. It was night. I liked the intimate feeling of sitting close to Robin in the dark, talking softly. I told her everything I knew about Sonny in Hollywood. She snorted when I mentioned *The Chief* series.

"It makes me crazy, the boys' club. They've got all that money to play with, they make crap, and we're begging for crumbs to do something worthwhile."

"You got your money," I said.

"What's that supposed to mean?"

"You got money from Hubbard."

"No strings attached."

"I'll bet." I thought about mentioning the cut over Sonny's eye, how Alfred and Dad were so sure Senior had picked that up from her tape. But something held me back.

"Look, Marty, we're all on the same page. We all want Sonny to be champ."

"You ever think Sonny wants to be something else?"

"What else?"

I didn't like the way she said it. As if he couldn't be something else. "Maybe we're pushing him for ourselves. Be the youngest champ. Be an Indian. Everybody's got their own idea of what you should be."

"Are you talking about Sonny or yourself?"

"Both of us, I guess. Who knows, maybe you, too."

"Maybe." She was quiet for a long time, but I kept my mouth shut. I knew she had more to say. Her voice barely made it over the grind and snarl of the old car. "I'm supposed to be in law school. Go into my father's firm. They think I'm fooling around, going through a boho phase before I grow up. I've got to get this documentary on the air."

"That's about what you want, not about Sonny."

"And what's your book about?"

"I'm not here as a writer, I'm here as Sonny's friend." It sounded so self-righteous that I started to squirm the minute I said it.

"You've been a good friend," she said. "I guess I'm just a producer."

I was glad I hadn't brought up the cut. But then I wondered if she was just soaping the soap man. After all, she was a producer. Then Sonny groaned and asked us to stop; he needed to barf.

By the time we were back on the road, Robin had a tape on. The soul-search was over. We talked about music.

Jake was sitting up in bed staring at the TV when we walked into his hospital room. He looked gaunt and gray. He was connected to beeping monitors. His arm was in a sling. He squinted at us.

"Sonny, you look bad," he said.

"You don't look so great yourself." He hugged Jake.

Jake wrinkled his nose. "You smell worse than you look."

"What happened?"

"Called for the Stump."

Sonny looked surprised. "That would do it. Nobody's called for the Stump since they killed your grandpa."

"Your great-great-grandpa," said Jake.

"What's the Stump?" asked Robin.

"Tell her," said Jake.

"Sometime."

"Now," said Jake. "See if you really know."

"Some kind of test?" asked Sonny.

"Maybe," said Jake.

There was a long pause. Sonny sat down, closed his eyes. Did he remember? Had he really been listening?

"Okay, but it don't mean anything," said Sonny.

Jake nodded. "I won't get no ideas you're an Indian."

Sonny spoke slowly: "Long ago, when Wahsdaywe, the Dog Who Laughs at Bears, was Chief of Chiefs, there was a fight between two subchiefs. It split the Nation. Over who owned a tree. One morning it was cut down. The subchiefs accused each other. Their Clans were ready to go to war, when Wahsdaywe said that it was a sign from the Creator.

"Nobody owns a tree. It's nature, like the earth, air, water. Belongs to everybody, together. Wahsdaywe said that what was left of the tree, the Stump, would become a treaty table, and any Moscondaga could call for the Stump in a crisis, and the whole Nation would work out the problem. The two subchiefs took the name Stump. They put their Clans together, and one of their offspring became Jake's great-great-great grandfather, who became a Running Brave."

"What happened to the Stump?" asked Jake.

"Still there. The white man outlawed the Stump when he outlawed the Running Braves. Called it pagan. The missionaries didn't like it for sure. Too much power to the people. Jake calling for a Stump is strong medicine."

Jake smiled and settled back into his pillow and closed his eyes. Sonny remembered.

At dawn we went out to the Res. We smelled the wet ashes as soon as we pulled off the paved county road. Jake's house was still standing, but the inside was gutted. The windows were black eyes. We poked around. Sonny found a broken bottle that smelled of gasoline. It must have been a quick, fierce fire. Sonny's old boxing trophies had melted down. An old leather backpack had dried into a wrinkled brown fist around a lump of melted crayons.

We were still picking through the rubble when a dozen men and boys sauntered up and surrounded us. They were casually carrying guns, like you see in news reports from Beirut or Palestine.

"How's Jake?" one of the men asked.

"Tough bird," said Sonny. "He'll be okay."

"You shouldn't be here."

"Live here," said Sonny.

"Bad time." He tilted his head. On the other side of the junkyard another small group stood, also casually carrying guns. They were looking at us. "Gonna go down."

"Maybe we got to do something," said Sonny.

"Like what?"

Sonny shrugged. "You think the casino's a bad idea?"

"Not even finished yet, look what it's doing."

"Maybe there's some middle way."

"What you got in mind?" They looked at each other and then back at Sonny. I had the feeling they wanted a leader.

But Sonny said, "Don't know yet."

They drifted away.

Robin headed back to New York, but she left her credit card so we could stay at a cheap motel near the hospital. Sonny bought a pair of running shoes and shorts and started jogging and exercising in the mornings. He said he was only doing it to feel better, he wasn't in training. But he was running hard.

We'd spend most of the day in the hospital with Jake, watching TV, talking. We watched an AIDS telethon to see Floyd (The Wall) Hall spar with Arsenio Hall and Geraldo Rivera, one round each. The Wall was kind of lame, no sense of humor, but he was huge, and not slow. When it was over, they asked him who he was going to fight next.

"Ask my man," he said.

Old Senior himself swaggered onto the set.

"There's a young man out there who thinks he should be champ because the spirits have told him so, and I'm not so sure he's wrong. We're waiting for you, Sonny Bear."

Jake cackled. "They need you to make them some big money."

"Not interested getting jerked around no more."

"If you beat him," I said, "you'd be champ."

"You think they're gonna let me beat him?"

* * *

Jake made us leave. "Nothing you can do here, Sonny. They'll try to kill you like they killed your great-great-grandfather."

"That's history, Jake."

"What you got except history?"

"What about you?"

"They'll leave me alone now."

"We should do something," said Sonny.

"You win the title, you got some power. Now you just get hurt."

We drove the pickup back to New York. We passed Stonebird in the distance. "I never did the solo."

"I'll go with you."

"It's a solo, no-brain." He began to laugh for the first time in weeks, laughing and laughing, and then crying, until we had to pull off the road.

After a while, Sonny wiped his eyes and looked at me. "What do we do now?"

We, he said.

"I'll figure something out on the way," I said.

He started laughing again. "Where'd I hear that before?"

26

THE GOVERNOR OF NEW YORK has his main office in Albany, the state capital, which is about halfway between Donatelli's Gym and the Res, but he spends a lot of time in an office in the World Trade Center in downtown Manhattan. When we got up to the desk in the reception area, a state trooper with a bull neck and a bulge under his green Kmart suit held up a palm.

"What can I . . . Hey, the Bear man." He leaned back in his swivel chair and threw a few jabs in the air. "Saw you get beat in Hillcrest a couple years ago."

"We're here to see the governor." Sonny's voice was deep, with the old hard edge. Pre-Hollywood.

"Ready to knock down the Wall?" It was that tone you use with children. The trooper wasn't taking Sonny seriously. I got nervous.

But Sonny was cool. "Ready to see the governor."

"Got an appointment? He's real busy on this Moscondaga thing."

"That's why we're here," said Sonny.

"He's got qualified people working on it."

"How about an Indian for a change?" I said.

The guard laughed at me through his skinny nose. "You don't look like an Indian to me."

Another trooper came up. "Governor's with some folks from Washington. Maybe come back tomorrow."

"People could start dying tomorrow," said Sonny.

"We're on the case, chief," said the first trooper. He made a big show of opening a newspaper to the sports section. His pal grinned. I could see Sonny starting to steam. "Later."

"Now." Sonny ripped the newspaper out of the trooper's hands.

"Whoa, boy." The trooper's face was red.

Sonny slapped the paper down on the desk. "Tell him Sonny Bear's here."

Both troopers were up now and their hands were on their guns. "You watch yourself, boy."

I stepped between them. "If anything happens on the Res and the governor finds out you didn't let Sonny in, you'll be back guarding toxic dumps."

They were happy to tangle with me instead of Sonny. "Don't smart-ass me, boy." The first one came around the desk and grabbed my shoulders. More troopers swarmed out of another office. "Get these jerks out of here."

"Hey." A guy with a notebook appeared. "Aren't you . . ."

"Sonny Bear!" I shouted. "Trying to get them to pay attention to a dangerous situation."

More reporters came out, and the troopers tried to get between them and Sonny, and then the two groups were jostling each other and the reporters were shouting at us over the fence of guards. It reminded me of Vegas.

"You here on the Reservation thing?"

"Big trouble," shouted Sonny.

"What are you going to do, Sonny?"

"Go back to the Res."

"Why?"

"See what I can do."

"Like what?"

"Get people talking to each other."

The troopers were pushing us out the door.

"Take it downstairs, boys."

"When you going up?" a reporter shouted.

"Today," said Sonny.

I said, "Today?"

"You got a date or something?" Sonny grinned as the troopers pushed us.

"Flying, driving?" one of the reporters asked.

"Running," said Sonny.

I looked at him. "Running?"

"You're going to run up to the Res?" asked a reporter. "That's hundreds of miles."

"Three hundred," said Sonny. "Nothing for a Running Brave."

"A who?"

"Did he say Running Brave?" They were all scribbling furiously, pushing their tape recorders toward Sonny. "Why?"

"Wake people up," said Sonny. "Make them see what's going on."

"What's going on?"

"Trying to screw the Nation again, set us against each other."

"Who?" A couple of the reporters were talking into their cellular phones.

"Government, white people."

We were out in the hallway now, and a wall of Kmart suits was pushing us into an open elevator.

"What's a Running Brave?"

"A warrior who can negotiate," yelled Sonny, "a diplomat who can fight, a . . ."

The elevator door closed on us.

"That was great, Sonny."

"Just starting." His eyes were bright, his shoulders were back.

"Now what?"

"This time we're going all the way."

"You're not going to run?"

"Your idea, man."

"To see the governor, not all this stuff."

Downstairs, the lunch-hour crowd jammed the lobby of the World Trade Center. Somebody yelled, "Sonny Bear!" and we were surrounded, people pushing scraps of paper at Sonny, trying to touch him.

"Gonna fight the champ?"

"You bet." He winked at me.

By the time we got out to the street, it was human gridlock, cops, workers, more reporters. The story must have been on the radio already. A TV truck pushed through the crowd, a correspondent standing on the roof, broadcasting live.

"A remarkable story is beginning to unfold here in New York's financial district as a young Native-American prizefighter, Sonny Bear . . ."

While Sonny gave interviews, I borrowed a cellular phone from a reporter. I needed a chase car for his run. Robin wasn't home, my folks were at work, Denise was at school, Henry was out of the gym. Finally, desperate, I called Alfred to borrow the HandiVan.

"Martin?" His voice sounded sharp. "Just saw you guys on TV. He really going to do it?"

"I think so."

"I'm coming."

"You sure you . . ."

"Meet you at the gym in an hour." He hung up.

I told Sonny.

"Good. You ready?"

"I can't run all the way."

"Just up to the gym."

"That's like eight, nine miles."

"You can do it." He took off.

What could I do? The first mile was murder: A stitch ran up and down my left side, and my

180

breath got caught in my rib cage, and my pants got caught in my crack. The second mile was actually easier; we were in Greenwich Village, where the streets were narrower and we had to slow down. A red TV truck pulled alongside me, and a woman stuck her mike out the window. "Can you tell us what . . ."

"Can't run . . . and . . . talk."

So they stopped, picked me up, and interviewed me in the truck as it followed Sonny up the middle of Manhattan.

"Sonny Bear carries the blood of the best, the warriors who can negotiate, the diplomats who can fight. . . ."

After that, every TV truck picked me up for a rolling interview. It was great. I felt like I was doing color commentary on the big game, watching Sonny run while I babbled on about why he was running.

I didn't have to run again until we were in Harlem. But by then it was only a few blocks to Donatelli's Gym. Alfred was waiting in the HandiVan. I fell in and we took off.

Alfred grinned at me. "Got my spare bladder bag, the shotgun and the thirty-eight. Let's rock 'n' roll, little brother."

27

'M TAKING NOTES again as Alfred keeps the HandiVan twenty-five feet behind Sonny on the highway heading north.

> . . . smooth stride . . . flows over the white stripe . . . inside himself, totally zoned . . . thinks only of mission, what need do to get there, what will do when arrive . . . Running Brave . . .

"You think he can run the whole way?" I ask.

"If the Hawk gives him a lift," snickers Alfred.

"You still don't buy that spiritual stuff."

"You know what I think."

"If it works, fine."

"You got it." He backhands my shoulder without taking his eyes off the road. "I think you're gonna be all right, Marty. A contender. Spoon always said so, but I was never sure till now."

"Dad said so?" There's a fist in my throat, my eyes sting.

"Never told you?"

"No."

"Probably did, but you missed the signal."

There are state troopers waiting for us at the entrance to the New York Thruway. One of them waves us down, a massive Black guy in a Smokey the Bear hat.

"No pedestrians." He jerks a thumb at Sonny, jogging in place.

Alfred shouts, "Sonny! Hop in."

I open the sliding door, and while Sonny climbs in, the Black Smokey pushes his face against a window. "What you got in there?"

"Guns, drugs, hypodermic needles," says Alfred. "I come to make your career."

"Smartmeat," snarls the Smokey. "We'll get you."

Alfred is laughing as he peels out. "He should've looked. I got guns, drugs, and needles. All legal, of course."

"You like this," I say.

"Love it. Action Jackson time." He looks over his shoulder at Sonny. "I'll pull off the next exit. How many miles a day you figure?"

"Fifty, a hundred? I don't know," says Sonny.

"Could take us five, six days to get there. The point you trying to make, man, is that people got to pay attention, okay, not that you got to win the Olympics, dig?"

I think Sonny might snarl back at him, but he just smiles and nods. There is something peaceful in his face.

Late in the day a helicopter appears overhead, beating the air with that brain-busting clatter. From the writing on its belly I see it's the weather chopper for a big New York radio station. I tune to their frequency.

One of those radio voices:

"Below us, a blue van is moving slowly up the road, trailing Sonny Bear on a mission that began hundreds of years ago when a band of Moscondaga warriors who called themselves the Running Braves became the feet and brains of their people."

A familiar voice:

"Sonny is a direct descendent of the last Running Brave, his great-great-grandfather. He's learned the secrets of that society, and he feels his time has come to help the Nation."

"That was Sonny's friend, Martin Witherspoon. But not everyone is so positive about this run. Joe Decker is a chief of the Moscondaga."

"Sonny Bear is not a representative of our people. He is a renegade out for himself. The Moscondaga know how to deal with a renegade."

"How?"

"By any means necessary."

At nightfall, Alfred bangs on the horn until Sonny drops back to my window. "Get in."

"I'm fine."

"I'm not. Gotta change my diapers, get some food. You got to sleep."

We pull into a truck stop, jammed with drivers. Some of them check us out but nobody bothers us. Alfred is gone a long time while Sonny and I eat.

"Alfred okay?" asks Sonny, which surprises me. He's not the sensitive type.

"Yeah. How 'bout you?"

"Hungry." He digs into his bowl of spaghetti. End of sensitive conversation.

Alfred rolls back with a plastic bag of underwear on his lap. "If you run in the dark, we'll never see what hits you."

Sonny nods. "Sleep in the van?"

"Tonight anyway."

I ask, "Tomorrow?"

"Out early, see what finds us," says Alfred.

"Finds us?"

"Count on it," says Alfred. "Good or bad, it's coming."

On our way out, one of the truck drivers yells, "Custer wins this time, kimo sabe."

Alfred wheels around, his hand inside his shirt on the .38, but Sonny never blinks, just keeps moving. Another driver yells "Shut up" to the first driver, but we're out of there.

"See, you also got your fans." Alfred chuckles. Action Jackson.

We find a space for the van among the rows of trucks parked for the night. The air hums with the sounds of radios and TV sets. Sonny wraps himself up in a blanket as if he's leftover food and goes to sleep without saying good night.

Alfred hands me the shotgun. "Wake me in two hours." He cranks his seat into recline, fusses with tubes and starts snoring.

The cold skin of the barrel sends shivers through my palm and up into my arm. This is real. There are people out there who don't want us to make it to the Res.

The shivers ripple out of my shoulder and into my chest. Fear can feel good, Jake says. Fear makes super sharp the senses of the Running Brave. He learned that from his grandfather and taught it to Sonny. But what's that got to do with me?

This is your run, too. Gonna deliver your message. Finish your book. Write it in blood if you have to.

Not mine, I hope.

How about Professor Marks' blood?

That'd be good.

"Huh?" Alfred is awake. Moonlight glints off the revolver in his hand.

"Sorry. Talking to myself."

"Keep your eyes open and your mouth shut."

"You really think there'll be trouble?"

"Nothing the three of us can't handle." He is snoring again.

* * *

187

Alfred shakes me awake at first light and gestures out my window at Sonny stick-dancing on the rutted black macadam of the parking lot. He wears only a jockstrap. He is barefoot.

He grunts softly each time the stick, a strip of plywood, bounces off an instep. He tracks it up into the pink-gray sky. The rising light glistens off his sweaty skin. He quicksteps under the tumbling stick, maneuvering himself into position on one foot to kick it back up with the other foot.

There is still Hollywood flab over the solid muscles of his abdomen, and I have seen him quicker and looser, but he looks good, powerful and graceful and confident in his body. He is getting back into shape.

Alfred and I watch for a long time. I could never dream of moving the way Sonny moves—I've been fighting fat my whole life. But Alfred was a fighter once, speedy and tough, and he was a very physical cop. I wonder how he feels now in the prison of his body.

Truck motors are coughing and sputtering around us by the time Sonny catches the stick behind his back and throws it away. He slides open the van door and hops in.

"Let's go."

"Breakfast," says Alfred.

"On the way. Stinks here."

Truck exhausts are pumping diesel fumes into the air. You can see what you're breathing.

"Progress," I say, "will kill you. The elders know what they're talking about."

"AIDS, TB, diabetes, booze," says Sonny, "kill you just as dead."

"We've got to take control of what we can," I say.

Alfred is chuckling as he pulls onto the highway. "Maybe Marty should run for chief."

I feel stupid until Sonny reaches from the back and squeezes my shoulder.

"Escort service," says Alfred, jerking a thumb behind us at a green Chevy. "State troopers." He points up through the windshield at a distant chopper. "Feds."

"Maybe they'll buy breakfast," I say.

"They'd love to," says Alfred. "At your friendly neighborhood slam." He taps the radio scanner until he finds an all-news station. We don't have to wait long.

"Violence has flared again on the Mos-condaga Reservation. One man was injured and thousands of dollars of construction materials destroyed when a bomb exploded at the site of a new gambling casino. The governor has promised to send state troopers to the Reservation to restore order. Elsewhere, . . ."

"Time to eat," says Sonny.

The green Chevy is replaced by a brown Ford when Alfred pulls off the highway. We decide to buy food at a convenience store and eat in the van. Alfred gets himself into his chair and rolls off to the bathroom while Sonny and I go inside.

The fat cracker behind the counter never takes his beady eyes off Sonny as he scoops up an armful of fruit and milk and cereal and juices. I pick up the newspapers, some packaged sandwiches and cookies, and large containers of coffee.

At the checkout, the cracker says, "Your money's no good here."

"We make a wrong turn?" I growl. "We're not in America?"

But I'm off base, and Sonny gets it right away. He puts out his hand. "Thanks."

The cracker pumps it. "Proud to meet you, Sonny. People got to stand up. Good luck to you."

The last time I will even think the word "cracker."

The papers don't have too much more on the Moscondaga story except a quote from one of the governor's aides who says that Sonny is only a boxer and that he represents no one on the Reservation. I read it out loud.

"Know which side the governor's on," says Alfred.

"The money side," says Sonny. "'S okay."

"Starting to sound like Jake," I say.

"'S okay," says Alfred. He's in a good mood. He finds a classic rock station and settles into driving. Sonny stretches out to digest. I scribble some notes while I check the sky and the road for latest developments.

Sonny has been running slow and smooth for almost two hours on a county blacktop that winds through old farms, when a gray stretch limo with a sky roof zooms out of a side road and pulls alongside. The roof slides back and a black leather cowboy hat pops up, followed by Elston Hubbard, Senior. He is grinning and signaling us to pull over.

"You think it's some kind of trick?"

"Count on it," says Alfred. He hits the horn for Sonny and eases the van onto the shoulder of the road.

Alfred makes a throat-clearing noise that sounds like a chain saw. "What do you want, Elston?"

"The best for everybody." He boosts himself out of the limo and onto its roof. He is totally in black leather. "Our boy is on the verge of capturing the imagination of this nation."

"Our boy?" I ask.

"His next fight belongs to me, remember?"

"Lay it out," snaps Alfred.

"A direct man. I can deal with that," says Hubbard. "This little run of yours, it's a ton of ink and air. The best buildup I've ever seen for a fight."

"With who?" asks Sonny.

"With the champ."

"What about Junior?" I ask.

"Good boy, my boy, but he don't have the Oh-Boy to sell a match with the Wall."

"Your own son." Alfred shakes his head.

"He'll get his shot," says Hubbard. "Now listen. Be a scramble, but we can schedule your fight in ten days. Pay-per-view. I'll have the suspension lifted.

"Sonny keeps running, every day in another town, he works out, meets the people and the press. I'll set up everything, the training sites, the motel rooms, food. Get you a phone and a fax for the van, a backup RV with a bathroom. Anything else you need, you got it."

"Sonny's running for a reason," I say, "not to promote a fight."

"Shut up," says Alfred. "The deal, Elston."

"You still tough, baby." Senior chuckles. "Okay. I want to promote a fight, Sonny wants to make a point. Together, we both get over. I get to be the fight king, he gets to be a Racing Beaver."

I can't believe this guy. "A Running Brave."

"Whatever. I'm not political."

"Where is this fight going to be?"

Hubbard smiles. He looks like a black crocodile when he smiles. "There is only one place in the cosmos where this can be held, gentlemens, and when I say the words you will lose your breaths."

"Hell?" I say.

Hubbard laughs. "That boy's mouth will

193

lead him to the penthouse or the outhouse. Gentlemens, this fight will be held at the grand opening of the Hiawatha Hotel and Casino."

"The what?" Alfred and I are a chorus.

"On the Moscondaga Reservation," says Hubbard. "We are talking about the greatest victory for the Native American since Little Big Horn."

"What do the chiefs say?" asks Sonny.

"When this goes down," says Hubbard, "you be the chief."

"May be nothing to be a chief of when you're done," I say.

He leans back and looks at us, cold eyes, no smile. "That's up to you."

28

RICHIE WAS WAITING for us outside the Fort Ruth Holiday Inn under the billboard: WEL-COME SONNY BEAR. I noticed that Sonny's name was bigger than Iron Pete Viera's had been. A good sign. But under his name it read: THE RUN TO THE TITLE. Bad sign.

"Classy, huh," said Richie. "Senior thinks of everything."

"Got to change it," I said. "It's not a run to the title. We're running to the Reservation, for a purpose. It's like a mission."

"'S okay," said Sonny. "We'll make our point when it's time. Now we're just chopping wood for the fire."

At four o'clock a crowd of several hundred whistled and clapped as Sonny jogged into the motel's banquet room and held out his hands for Alfred to tape. I really missed my laptop. Got to get this down. Only Day Two of this amazing run, and it feels like just another work-out in the gym. That's something to write about, when history feels like everyday.

Sonny stretched and shadowboxed to loosen up, sparred with two different partners, then hit the heavy bag and speed bag mounted on portable metal stands. Richie drilled him through his exercises. Once I thought I heard Richie say "Oy, vay."

I didn't get a chance to talk to Sonny that night. He went right to sleep after dinner, and Alfred hurried to his room to give himself an enema, clean his tubes and bags.

I wandered downstairs. Richie was supervising the sparring partners taking down the ring. No time to talk, either. "Four o'clock tomorrow in the Ramada Inn, Breitenburg Falls. Go with the flow, kid."

Day Three.

. . . *Robin and crew in Ramada Inn parking lot . . . band from local H.S. . . . strike up Rocky theme as Sonny approaches. . . . Each band member wears red ribbon . . . shivers in January cold . . .*

. . . Robin looks thinner, feverish, says "I'm calling the film Red Ribbons. *Title evokes trails of Indian blood, as well as . . ."*

. . . I ask, "Where'd they get the ribbons?"

"It's a very poor high school. Senior paid for the bus that brought them here."

Day Four.

Sonny looks so strong, gliding over the road, mile after mile with that long, clean stride, through the wind and a snow flurry, his hair streaming behind him, in light sweats and no gloves. I wonder if he imagines himself a Running Brave who has trained for this journey since childhood, thousands of miles in preparation, a hero who has eaten vegetables and grains and the flesh of swift creatures. Is he thinking of hawks?

Although I cannot see them, I imagine his eyes fierce with his determination to reach his destination. He carries the hopes and the fate of his people. Should I try to get ahead of him and actually look at his eyes? That's journalism, not creative writing.

"What you mumbling?" asked Alfred.

"You know the first athletes in America were Indian runners?"

"This *Jeopardy?*"

"In 1680, the runners carried messages coded into carved sticks and knotted strings to the Pueblos. It was a revolt against the Spanish."

"How'd they do?"

"Kicked ass."

Alfred laughed. "How come they didn't teach us that in school?"

"In 1890, runners went to Washington to tell the Indian side of the massacre at Wounded Knee."

"Do any good?"

I pointed at Sonny. "Still at it."

Sometimes Richie set up the training camp in a community center or a school auditorium. The crowds grew at every stop. So did the media. They began following us in a chartered bus. Same questions: Why are you doing this? How old are you? Think you can really knock down the Wall?

I got to talk to Richie only once, caught him alone staring at the wall after a workout. I stood quietly until he turned to me and said, "John L. would of loved all this. He talked about Sonny a lot. You know that pillow Sonny gave him? I stuck it in his coffin just before they closed it. Rabbi would've gone nuts, but I figured, hey, who knows who's in charge up there?"

When he realized that tears were streaming down his face, he turned away, and growled, "Don't you got something to do, pencil-boy?"

I decided it was not the time to bring up the five hundred dollars he still owed me.

On the fifth day, Dave the Fave showed up to spar, and to do his "Sonny's Run" rap. We were on the news every night. The governor said it was just too bad people were listening to a boxer instead of their elected officials, and Hubbard said it would be the biggest fight in history.

Dick, the silver-haired TV guy who had helped us in Las Vegas, flew in for a special network interview. Afterward, he said to me, "Watch yourself, Marty. There are people who don't want Sonny to make it."

"Like who?"

He raised his hands. "A word to the wise, *capisce?*"

Good Morning, America showed up on Day Six with Sonny's mom. They interviewed them together, on a wooden deck overlooking a lake. It was so cold they had to surround them with silver foil and beam heat lamps at them.

Alfred and I watched on a monitor inside a tent. Sonny's mom was beautiful and articulate. She looked like she could be his older sister. Sonny seemed a little uncomfortable, but she did all the talking. About how hard it was for Sonny growing up without a dad and how they moved around a lot, but that he had the strength of his two cultures, red and white. She managed to hold up some of the jewelry she designed, and get in a few plugs for Sweet Bear's Kiva craft shops and the new line of "Tomahawk Kid" Indian-style sweat clothes.

It wasn't until the very end that the interviewer got around to asking Sonny if he was excited about his chance of becoming the youngest heavyweight champion in history.

It took him so long to answer that Alfred

and I glanced at each other, but then he finally squinted down the barrel of the camera and said, "I'm sure my mom feels the same way. There's nothing we could make or do as individuals that would be as important as what we could do as members of the Moscondaga Nation."

"Oooo-eee." Alfred gave me an elbow. "Hawk been whispering to that boy."

"See, you're starting to believe," I said.

"Always believed. In whatever works."

Day Seven.

Alfred is at the wheel when the bullet ricochets off the roof of the van.

It's dawn, Sonny is outlined against the horizon, a perfect target, and we hear a crack, like a branch snapping, and the ping of a spent cartridge bouncing off the van. I'm not sure what it is, but Alfred knows right away. He hits the horn and guns the van, pulling alongside Sonny.

"Door," Alfred shouts to me, and as I slide it open, he shouts to Sonny, "In."

"Got to keep going."

"If you go down it's over."

Sonny throws himself through the door onto a pile of blankets and clothes on the floor of the van.

Alfred unhooks the phone and flips it into my lap. "Call the local cops."

"Call the Res," says Sonny.

"They're the ones trying to kill you."

"They wouldn't of missed," says Sonny. "Call Jake."

Jake has only one question. "Where you at?" When I tell him he hangs up.

Sonny pulls off his shoes and flops backward. He is snoring before Alfred pulls over. "You drive now."

I drive the HandiVan and Alfred leans out the passenger window, the shotgun balanced on his knees, his old police revolver in his hand. Steering the van, I think I'm in the middle of a western movie, driving the Butterfield stage through Indian country.

Only in this flick it's the Indians coming to the rescue.

29

FIFTEEN MILES FROM Sparta I spotted the first war party, half a dozen Moscondaga standing back to back in the bed of Jake's pickup, their rifles and shotguns bristling.

Alfred yelled, "Sonny, get in!"

"They're us," Sonny yelled back, without breaking stride. He gave the warriors the Running Brave fist. They silently raised their weapons.

Jake pulled up in the pickup. Two Moscondaga clambered up on top of the HandiVan. Jake dropped back and fell in behind us.

Another truck filled with Moscondaga riflemen cut in front of Sonny. Then two Indians on motorcycles, shotguns strapped to their backs, roared out of the trees to flank Sonny.

"You believe this?" asked Alfred.

"Maybe Hubbard sent them," I said. "For the documentary."

"Don't be too hip to be happy. Chills up my spine, and I hardly got one."

I had chills, too, but I was too hip to tell him.

For the next ten miles, our caravan grew, cars and trucks and motorcycles. At the Sparta city limits two warriors on horseback, one with a long hunting rifle on his back, the other with a bow and a quiver of arrows, galloped out of a farm road and took the point.

The phone rang. Hubbard. "I'm here in beautiful downtown Sparta with the governor. Keys to the city, a medal from the state. Just make sure our boy's cool." He hung up.

We arrived in Sparta in the middle of the afternoon. It was the first big city we'd been in since New York, a week ago, and it seemed huge and concrete. The streets were lined with cheering, waving people; they must have come from all over that part of the state. Most of them were wearing red ribbons. There were red ribbons on every tree and telephone pole. A band was playing. In the center of downtown the governor was on a reviewing stand with Hubbard and a montage of faces I recognized from TV news. There was a grove of cameras on the stand, some facing us, some facing the famous faces.

An enormous banner, red with white lettering, hung across the main street:

SPARTA SALUTES SONNY BEAR

We swept through the city, guns pointed out, surrounded by warriors. Sonny didn't even look at the reviewing stand. Just kept running, right out of town toward the Reservation. Can't get cooler than that. I caught a glimpse of Hubbard and his famous faces, frozen.

There were roadblocks and troopers and clattering choppers overhead as we approached Stonebird. No one tried to stop us. Sonny headed right into the Reservation, through the green tunnels, running past the trailers and the junkyard and the Longhouse, until he reached the Stump.

I'd never paid it much attention, even when I was getting into Moscondaga myths and all. The Stump was about four feet high, but too thick to get your arms completely around it. The top was flat as a table and polished shiny by centuries of people rubbing it for luck.

Sonny leaped up on the Stump.

He waited for a long time, until the caravan had stopped, until hundreds of Moscondaga, people from Sparta, media, police, the governor and his entourage, had climbed out of their cars and trucks, had dismounted from their horses and hogs, and formed an enormous circle around the Stump. Robin's crew was down front, aiming up at Sonny.

"No pictures," he said.

"You must be joking."

Slowly, patiently, Sonny said, "The wisdom keepers believed that photographs could steal your powers." His voice sounded different, not deeper or older or anything I could name, just different.

"You can't really believe that." Robin's eyebrows nearly lifted off her face.

"I have to trust the wisdom keepers."

They stared at each other a long time before Robin said, "Cap it."

The camerawoman made a face at the sound guy, but she covered the camera lens.

It was very quiet when Sonny spoke.

"My name is Dawadoh. I am the son of Answedaywe, daughter of Oktedowe who was son of Lamagha, who was son of Hodanoh, who some have thought was the last of the Running Braves.

"This was not true. The secrets of the society were passed down to his grandson,

Garanguthwa, my great-uncle, who passed them to me. I claim the Stump as a Running Brave with a message for the Nation."

Decker strode forward, an Uzi in his hand, five casino goons behind him. "He's not even full-blood."

Jake said, "His mother was the daughter of a Chief."

"You got to be full-blood to claim the Stump," said Decker.

"Says who?" shouted one of the riflemen who had ridden on top of the van.

One of the goons said, "Butt out."

Cartridges hammered into chambers, *chick-chack*; magazines slapped up into automatic weapons. People were pushing children down. The crowd was too dense for anyone to run away. The camerawoman slipped off her lens cap.

Sonny raised his arms in a gesture that held the peace just long enough for the crowd to part, for people to make way for an old man hobbling with a carved stick. The Chief of Chiefs of the Moscondaga Nation. He raised the stick. His voice was rumbly.

"Prepare the Stump. Dawadoh will speak."

Alice Benton, the Clan Mother, rushed forward and circled the Stump, sprinkling shredded leaves from two old leather bags. She lighted the leaves and chanted.

When she finished, Sonny leaned down to take a deep breath from the curling smoke. He looked around, nodding and making eye contact with the people around the Stump. Decker and his men looked down, trying to avoid looking back into his eyes, but they couldn't. The force of Sonny's will made them acknowledge him.

He spoke:

"First, I apologize for speaking in English. I do not know our language well enough to make myself understood in it, to be sure that I am saying what I mean to say. Someday I hope I will be able to speak it well. I claim the Stump because I think this can be a good time or a bad time for our people, and it is up to us to choose."

I thought Jake's wrinkled cheeks were glistening. Tears?

"The casino is not a good thing or a bad thing unless we make it one or the other. If we take control so the money goes to the Nation, if we are not greedy, if we remain a family, we will be all right. Otherwise it will destroy us."

Someone shouted out, "You got a plan?"

"It is not for me to plan for the entire Nation. We should meet in the Longhouse, as our grandfathers and our grandmothers did, and decide together. I can only plan for myself. I will not fight at the casino until the Nation tells me to."

"You got no choice," yelled Decker. "You signed a contract."

"We all got a contract with the Creator," said Sonny. "That comes first."

The Chief of Chiefs raised his stick. "We will go into the Longhouse. Garanguthwa and Dawadoh will join us. All those who are not Moscondaga must leave the Reservation now."

He turned and walked toward the Longhouse. Sonny jumped off the stump and took Jake's arm. They followed the Chief, and then the members of the Council of Elders followed them. Grumbling, Decker fell into step with the subchiefs and the Clan Mothers.

Alfred and I drove back to Sparta. Near the city's main medical center we found a motel that had good wheelchair access and a huge bathroom. I stretched out on one of the beds and channel surfed. We were all over the waves, although mostly they got the story wrong. They called Sonny a young chief, which he certainly was not, of the Iroquois, to which the Moscondaga do not belong, and they had Sonny running to emphasize the exploitation of the Indians since Columbus, whom he has never mentioned. And they didn't go into the issues on the Res. Too complicated for their freeze-dried heads.

But the pictures were sensational, blimp shots, chopper shots, hand-held, minicam. I had no idea what we looked like until I saw it on TV. The caravan had stretched for miles behind us: first the Moscondagas who were guarding us, the whole Nation it seemed, carrying everything from AK-47s to ceremonial tomahawks; and there were other Nations, the Onondaga were there and the Mohawks; and there were biker clubs, the Galloping Ghosts, the Rumson Riders; there was a Baptist church group in a yellow school bus and old folks in Silverstreams and Winnebagos and eco types on their bicycles and Jaguars and Rent-a-Wrecks and muscle cars; and every brand of cop and news-hound and a county beauty pageant float and a beer truck and ice cream wagons; but the best were the overhead shots of the HandiVan, the Indians crouched on the roof searching for snipers and Alfred hanging out the window with his shotgun and, there he is, peering through the windshield, a heroic brown face with little round glasses sliding down his nose. I gave myself the fist.

Hubbard called. He invited Alfred and me to dinner. I said I'd get back to him as soon as Alfred returned from a meeting. I wasn't going to tell him that Alfred was in the tile temple Roto-Rootering his personal plumbing.

Hubbard took us to the best restaurant in town, or at least the fanciest, all leather and wood, on top of an office building with a 360-degree view of the city. In daylight you could probably see the Res. He was wearing a pin-striped gray banker's suit.

"First of all, gentlemens, a small token of thanks for a job well done." He started peeling off bills. Alfred's pile was higher than mine, and if I was counting right, mine was about $10,000. Five Armani suits.

"We don't work for you, Elston," said Alfred. "We get our cut from Sonny's end."

"Up to you make sure there is an end."

"That's what they're talking about in the Longhouse," said Alfred.

"How serious all that stuff?" He looked at me.

"Sonny believes he is a Running Brave on a mission to save his people," I said. "It comes before any fight."

Hubbard cursed. "You got any idea how much bread I spread to make this happen? The boxing commissions, the casino authority, the federal agencies . . ."

"Should've just bribed the Creator," I said.

"I am losing patience with your big . . ."

"Shut up," said Alfred. "Why we here?"

"I got to be sure your boy shows up for the fight."

"Can't promise," said Alfred. He pushed both piles of money back to Hubbard. "He's his own man. Better pray the Hawk leads him into the casino Friday night."

"If he does fight, what kind of condition he gonna be in?"

Alfred shrugged. "What do you care?

You've got it locked up either way."

Hubbard shook his head. "You may not believe this, but I love that boy."

"I don't believe it," said Alfred. "After he knocked you and Junior out?"

"I forgive a boy's got the goods," said Hubbard. "He could be a great champion and make me rich beyond my dreams."

"Now I believe it," said Alfred.

Jake called us around noon to get back to the Res. The Council would be coming out soon. Indians at a roadblock checked our names and IDs. Mostly media on their list.

It was early afternoon when they came out, blinking in the harsh light, a little unsteady on their feet from all those hours of sitting. The Chief of Chiefs led the way, then the members of the Council, the Clan Mothers, the subchiefs. There were no guns. Sonny and Jake walked with arms linked.

The chief waited while the TV cameras set up.

"This is what has been decided by the Nation. When every Moscondaga who wants work has a job, the boxing will go on. The hotel

213

and casino will be allowed to operate after a contract is signed making the Nation a partner, with a percentage of the profits. *Dah-neh-hoh.* That is all."

The reporters began to yell out questions, but the chief turned his back and walked away.

"Sonny, what do you say?"

"You heard the chief." He smiled. *"Dah-neh-hoh."*

30

N A QUIET, EMPTY room that smelled of freshly cut lumber, Alfred slowly, carefully taped Sonny's hands, packing extra gauze over the middle right knuckle. Jake kneaded the muscles of Sonny's thighs and calves, and I worked on the knotted muscles of his shoulders and back.

"Stick and move," said Alfred. "The Wall's strong. Be hard to hurt him till he's tired."

"He's got a short right uppercut," said Richie. "Likes to head-hunt."

"Don't let him inside," said Alfred.

Richie said, "When you think you can slip off the uppercut, when his arm comes up, you hook to his liver, hook to his chest, when he drops that arm, hook to his jaw."

"Take your time," said Alfred.

"Patient, then pounce," said Richie.

Sonny looked at me. "What do you say, Marty?"

Richie said, "He don't know, he . . ."

215

"Writing Brave," said Sonny. "He knows."

I said it fast before I lost my voice. "Sludge."

Alfred and Jake looked at each other. They didn't know; they weren't there. But Richie began to shake his head.

"That's what I think," said Sonny. "Take his best shot early, then put him away."

"No, no, don't be crazy." Richie slathered Vaseline on the old scar over Sonny's left eye. "You got to take down the Wall slow, brick by brick."

"Won't mean anything 'less I stretch him out."

I said, "Hook . . . twenty-one. Right . . . ten. Hook . . . five."

"Bingo," said Sonny.

Richie began to jabber, but Jake held up his hand. "How you feel?"

"I can smell the salt in his sweat," said Sonny. He winked at me.

"Sounds ready," said Jake.

"Let's do it," I said.

Alfred spun around and wheeled toward the door.

Outside, we smacked into a wall of blinding lights and deafening sounds. I staggered, steadied myself against the back of Alfred's chair. Drums, whistles, stamping feet. Colored spotlights blazed from the unfinished ceiling of the Hiawatha Hotel and Casino.

Alfred was in the lead, clearing the way, his cop's eyes punching through the neon haze, his hand inside his jacket. I was right behind him, carrying the buckets. I glanced over my shoulder.

Sonny looked good, swaggering down the aisle, banging his big red gloves together, whipping his black ponytail from side to side against his bare shoulders. He looked nasty, wired, ready to rock. He had run and he had spoken and he had negotiated, and now it was time for the Running Brave to fight.

I felt great. My senses were super sharp. I could smell Denise's perfume and I could hear Professor Marks scratching notes on his program—he better not be writing his own book about Sonny—and I could see Robin giving signals to her crew. I will remember everything, a gift from the Creator to a Writing Brave.

And what happens next? Will the truce on the Res hold? Will the casino honor its treaty with the Moscondaga? Will we ever find out who fired that shot? Will Robin make her movie, will we all get rich and famous? Will I flunk out of school? That's another book.

Richie kicked me from behind; "Keep moving," and I stumbled and hit Jake with a bucket. "Sorry." He grinned. "'S okay," and I said, "He's going to win, I know he's going to win," and Alfred said, "He already won, Marty. This is just the fight."

Turn the page for a sneak preview of the
next novel in Robert Lipsyte's groundbreaking
The Contender boxing saga,

WARRIOR ANGEL

SONNY LOOKED AWFUL, DRUGGED, A ROBOT. He lurched out to the center of the ring, hands down, chin out. If Crockett hadn't been stiff with fear, he could have marched up and nailed him, ended the fight right then.

Look at those idiot managers, jumping up and down, yelling at Sonny to lift his hands, go after Crockett, chop that lard ass down. Do they want him to lose, or are they as stupid as the boxing writers say? They aren't much older than Sonny, punks who worked for that slimeball Hubbard. Why did Sonny let them in? Because he's losing his grip. Because he doesn't know who his real friends are. Because he needs me.

The crowd screamed for action.

PJ slipped onto the couch next to Starkey. "That was so cool, the way you got out of Circle. Which is the one you're rooting for?"

"Red trunks," said Starkey.

Roger plopped down. "Crockett's scared. Why doesn't Bear just put him away?"

Because I want all this to end, thought Starkey, thinking for Sonny, because I want to be free, to go back to sleep, to be alone.

A voice on the TV cut through the murk.

3

"Navy, stick, stick and move, Navy."

"That guy used to train Sonny," said Starkey, "back when Alfred, Henry, and Jake were still in his corner." They didn't need to know all this. But he couldn't stop talking about Sonny. "That was all before Hubbard's punks took over."

"You know so much about him," said PJ.

"Starkey is obsessed with Sonny Bear," said Roger.

"We're not allowed to diagnose in the Family Place," said PJ.

"It's an observation, not a diagnosis," said Roger. "There are people who fixate on stars because of a lack in their own—"

"Shut up!" The words came out like straight rights and shut Roger right up.

A jab bounced off Sonny's forehead, just enough to shake him, not enough to hurt. Starkey felt pressure over his left eye.

Sonny looked blank, unfocused. Starkey imagined that Sonny's mind was wandering, seeing faces from his past floating in the crowd, attaching themselves to bodies, then moving on, like masks on strings. Mom and Doll and Robin, Alfred and Marty and Jake.

4

He imagined that Sonny felt dreamy now, surprised that his body could move on its own, as if it were acting out highlights from old fights. Remember how we kept moving to the left on Boatwright so he couldn't pull the trigger on his jab, in and out on Velez, who was dangerous but dumb.

One of the TV commentators said, "Crockett's got too much reach. Sonny has to move inside if he wants to win this."

"He's having trouble just keeping his hands up," said the other one.

"Sonny, look out," screamed the idiots in the corner.

Suddenly, Sonny was on the ring floor and the referee was pushing Crockett into a neutral corner. Starkey tried to feel Sonny's shock and pain, but felt only numbness. Was that all Sonny was feeling too?

The steel drums smothered the sound of the referee's count, but Starkey could see him mouthing the numbers. "Two . . . three . . . four . . ."

"Up, Sonny, get up," screamed Starkey.

"Stay down, Sonny," said Roger. "You get up, it's just more of the same."

He wanted to slug Roger, as big as he was. He started to rise, felt PJ's body stiffen. He held the tension for a beat and thought, If Roger is a member of the Legion of Evil, if he is the adversary sent up from Hell to test me on this Mission, does it make sense to engage him now? Do you beat the devil early or late?

The bell rang.

"Sonny is saved by the bell," snorted Roger.

You, too, thought Starkey. I will not engage you now. This is about Sonny right now, not about me.

Hands dragged Sonny to his stool, snapped an ampule under his nose, poured ice water on his head, dropped a cube down the front of his trunks, massaged his arms and legs.

The camera moved in. Starkey saw the boom mike, a fuzzy fat gray caterpillar hovering over Sonny's head, picking up the conversation in his corner.

"Wake up, Sonny." The trainer was slapping his face.

"What's your name?" A man in a suit and tie. The ring doctor.

"Sonny Bear."

"Where are you?"

"Las Vegas."

"Who you fighting?"

"Navy Crockett."

The doctor shrugged and walked away.

One of the idiot managers said, "Sonny, you got to back off—"

But the other idiot said, "In his face, get right up in Crockett's face—"

And then the trainer said, "Tie him up."

Too many voices in Sonny's ear, Starkey thought, when all he needs is mine. He said, "Just hang on."

"For dear life." Roger laughed.

The bell rang.

Bolder now, Crockett marched right up and fired a jab. Some distant memory must have jogged Sonny to slip the punch, let it fly harmlessly over his shoulder, to ram a short right uppercut into Crockett's soft belly.

"Huuunh." Crockett doubled over, his chin slamming into Sonny's shoulder. Sonny grabbed him, pulled him into a clinch. Crockett wrenched loose and stumbled away.

The fear was back. Crockett circled again. The movie stars and rappers and ballplayers stamped their cowboy boots and chanted,

"Son-nee, Son-nee."

Behind them, to the steel-drum beat, voices from the cheaper seats chanted, "Nay-vee, Nay-vee."

Starkey could sense that Sonny's murkiness never completely cleared and that he never quite connected with his body, even when he got his hands up and began to move his feet. Twice he caught Crockett coming in with sharp jabs. The second time he managed to land a hook as Crockett was backing away. It startled Crockett, and he tripped over his feet, falling on his backside. He was up again before the referee could start the count, but he stayed away from Sonny for the rest of the round.

The crowd began to boo through the middle rounds as the fight fell into a pattern. Crockett would circle until he gathered enough courage to attack. He might land a jab or two, even a brief flurry of punches, but Sonny would trap his arms and step into a clinch.

The referee broke them apart as quickly as he could, "No hugging—fight," but Crockett couldn't stop Sonny from clinching.

One of the TV commentators said, "Navy's too slow, too set in his ways to figure this out."

"He's a classic plodder willing to absorb punches to give some back," said the other. "But Sonny's hardly mounting any offense at all. Wasn't this supposed to be a just a little tune-up fight for the champ?"

At the beginning of the tenth, Starkey sensed Sonny's murk beginning to lift, like a stage curtain slowly rising. He could see that Sonny felt it first in his arms, lighter, then in his feet, moving faster. Sonny snapped three straight jabs into Crockett's face, driving him back across the ring, and as the crowd began to roar, he slammed a left hook into Crockett's jaw and a vicious short right into his heart. Crockett fell against the ropes, his elbows snagged on the top strand. The crowd was on its feet as Sonny lowered his head and pounded Crockett's soft gut.

"Kill the body and the head will die," shouted Starkey.

Roger snickered. "Where you hear that dopey stuff?"

Starkey started to rise, but PJ squeezed his arm and he settled back down. It was in The Book. Mr. Donatelli had spoken those words to Alfred, who had passed them on to Sonny.

9

Can't react to Roger, not now.

Crockett had nothing left, he was in no condition to box for twelve rounds, and he sucked air and circled until the final bell sounded. The crowd was booing and whistling. It got louder after the ring announcer pulled down the mike and read the judges' cards.

Split decision. Sonny wins, retaining the title.

Starkey felt sweet warm relief fill his chest.

"Crockett got robbed," said Roger. "And your guy is almost as screwed up as you are."

"Get lost," snapped Starkey.

Roger stood up. "Make me, psycho pup."

Defining moment, now or never. Starkey stood up. He tried to imagine what Sonny would do, but before he could even think it through, the heel of his hand shot out and slammed into Roger's nose. Roger sat down hard, blood leaking between his fingers.

Roger whimpered. "I'm gonna tell—"

"And I'll say you bothered me," said PJ. "Now get lost, toad."

PJ didn't wait for Roger to leave before she sat down and hugged Starkey. He was too surprised to resist. Besides, he knew Roger would snitch to Dr. Raphael that he had hit him and they'd send a counselor up.

Then I can get back to my room and send Sonny another message. He closed his eyes and wrote it in his mind: *Dear George Harrison Bayer, Saw you on TV after the fight. That look in your eyes, like it's hopeless. It's not. Hang on. I'll be there as soon as I can. Warrior Angel.*